Winter
TAKES ALL

PARANORMAL DATING AGENCY

NY TIMES & USA TODAY BESTSELLING AUTHOR
MILLY TAIDEN

Published By
Latin Goddess Press, Inc.
Winter Springs, FL 32708
http://millytaiden.com
Winter Takes All
Copyright © 2018 by Milly Taiden
Cover by: Willsin Rowe
Edited by: Tina Winograd
Formatting by Glowing Moon Designs

—For my readers.
Love will find you in the ends of the earth!

WINTER TAKES ALL

Where's a curvy girl with a love of snowy mountains and cold, crisp air to find a man who'll light her fire? Gerri Wilder knows just the place and most certainly the right shifter. Promising a guy with warm hands and a hot body to keep Juliet Taylor cozy on those long Alaskan nights, the sexy scientist has to wonder if the renowned matchmaker's idea of a hot date will waddle up to her door wearing a tuxedo made of feathers.

Leaving home after a heart-wrenching tragedy, Tevrik Awulf has stayed hidden away in the most remote corner of Alaska for nearly fifteen years. Guilt, loneliness, and snow his only companions, he refuses to believe that any woman would ever live in a shack in the middle of the frozen tundra, let alone that the mate for him will fall out of the sky. Obviously, his friend's had way too much caffeine.

Threatened by an avalanche, Tevrik finds himself catching the most gorgeous woman he's ever laid eyes on as she falls right out of the sky. With every hour that passes, Juliet sinks deeper into his soul and becomes part of his very existence until he's wonders how he ever lived without her. The world stops when Juliet goes missing. With the need to find, protect and tear apart whoever has taken her, Tevrik's suppressed alpha roars to life. Can this lonely warrior let go of the past that haunts him or will he lose the only woman who can give him a future worth living?

ONE

Juliet held back tears. Tried to anyway. She was such a damn romantic, she was surprised she wasn't bawling her eyes out. She watched as her best friend Raven was swept from the singles auction into the limo where her soul mates secretly awaited her. It was the sweetest thing and she loved every second of it.

Juliet heaved, swallowing a sob of happiness. Raven was the best friend anyone could be blessed with. How many friends would've flown two thousand miles, put their life in danger, and almost died, to rescue you? Yeah, not many. That's why Raven was so deserving of love and happiness with two of the hottest men on the planet.

She bounced on her toes and waved as the limo drove away, then stood there watching the tail lights fade into the darkness. She sighed. Was it considered wrong to be jealous of your bestie in the love department? Juliet would never try to take one of the guys from Raven, but why couldn't she just find one. Out of seven billion people on the damn planet, she wanted only one who was made for her.

You've got to go where the men are, Raven constantly told her. There were men in the Arctic region among chest-high snow and icebergs. Just not many. And unfortunately, Juliet had probably met them all and no love connection.

The charity ball and singles auction continued inside the mansion. Juliet was no longer in the celebratory mood required for the event. She blew out a breath, dabbed at her wet eyes, and turned—

"Oh," she said, startled there was a woman standing behind her. "I'm so sorry. I didn't know anyone was still out here."

"They make a lovely trio, don't they," the woman said, nodding toward the distant limo.

Juliet's heart twisted, but she smiled through it. "Yes, the perfect trio."

The woman put her hand out. "I'm Gerri Wilder."

Juliet shook the delicate, flawless hand. "Juliet Taylor. I'm a friend of Raven's."

Gerri slipped her arm around Juliet's and guided her through the front mansion doors. Juliet was about to object, wanting to go home and cry in a half-gallon of vanilla bean Ben & Jerry's and watch The Proposal for the thousandth time.

But Gerri said, "I set up Ice and Frost with Raven. I knew they'd be a great match. That's what I do. Paranormal Dating Agency matchmaker extraordinaire at your service. I knew right away they were the perfect ones to give her quite a few of the *O*s." Gerri smirked at Juliet.

Did she really just mention orgasms? Was she being pranked? Hidden cameras somewhere?

If Juliet had been drinking, it would've snorted out her nose. Matchmaker? In the twenty-first century?

"You mean that you work at one of those dating sites that put people together based on their traits?" She'd thought about trying a couple of those online hook-up websites, but heard they were just that— hook-ups for one night. She didn't know if that was true or not, but that wasn't her.

She was the one-woman, one-man forever type. Just like in all her romance books and movies.

Happily-ever-after was what she was after. In her mid-thirties, she was ready to share her life with someone who loved her. A huge bonus would be if the man liked living in nature where it was cold. Where they could sit on a mountain and watch the sun rise as little chipmunks tittered at their feet.

Okay, now she was getting a little sickening with all the mushy stuff. If she were to write a book, it would be one big romantic cliché—*You had me at hello. We'll always have Paris.*

"Are you here with a date or are you part of the auction?" Gerri asked, snapping Juliet out of her mini pity party.

She laughed. Of course, she was single. Was she glowing in love's aura? Think not. "I am being auctioned off. My mom's doing actually. I tried to get out of it, but she was not having any of that." She quickly added, "Not that I really wanted out, it's for a good cause and all. I'm just not expecting to find a match." Gerri dipped a brow at her. Juliet replied, "Really, if or when Mr. Right shows up, I'm ready and waiting, I'm just not holding my breath I find him at a single's auction. Besides, I've got a great career going."

Gerri stopped at the back of the ballroom with Juliet in tow. "You haven't given up on love then?

Just waiting for the right person to come along, hmmm?"

Yes, she loved her job and what she did at the National Snow and Ice Data Center, but she wasn't so driven that she wasn't open to new ideas or new experiences. Hell, she'd even date a shifter. Raven's men were dragon shifters and they treated Raven like a queen. She'd just make sure her man wasn't a weird shifter like a gopher or prairie dog. Were there even shifter prairie dogs? She couldn't imagine having prairie puppies where they'd shift and hide *under* the sofa, they were so tiny.

"I completely believe in love. My parents are like horny teenagers even after being married for over thirty-five years. Raven and her men are very much in love. So, yes, I believe in it," she replied to Gerri. "I'd like to think there's give and take in a relationship. As long as I don't do all the giving."

Gerri laughed with her. "So, you're okay with something different or new and by that I mean, would a shifter be acceptable, one that would give you lots of…attention, love, and orgasms?"

"Whoa," Juliet said. Now she was catching on. "Thank you for your assistance, Ms. Wilder. But I'll find a significant other on my own. I don't want to waste your time." And this woman had to be batshit crazy. Who talked about orgasms with a complete stranger?

"What makes you think I'd be wasting my time?" Gerri asked, a little indignant. "I have never been wrong before, nor would I be with you."

Well, if she hadn't just put her foot in her mouth. "I didn't mean to imply that you don't know what you're doing. Raven and Ice and Frost are great together—"

"But you don't think I can find you the man who is perfect for you?" Gerri finished for her.

Yes.

"No," Juliet stumbled along, "it's just that I'm so picky when it comes to men. . ." She didn't know how to dig out of the hole she'd created. "Okay. I'll tell you what, Ms. Wilder. If you find me my perfect husband, I'll be the first person to shout to the rooftops how amazing you are."

Gerri smiled—a little wickedly. It was kinda creepy and made her wonder if she'd just doomed herself.

"I'm sorry, dear. I just love a good challenge," Gerri said.

Oh, shit. What had she done? Now was she expected to go on a million first dates until the right man came by? She groaned inwardly. "Well," she said with reluctance, "I'll be leaving in a bit for Alaska. I have routine work there."

Gerri perked up. "Alaska? How fascinating. What do you do?"

"I'm a geologist," Juliet straightened her back. "I work for the national snow agency." That was how she explained her company to the general public. Better than spitting out the initials NSIDC. That was a mouthful. "And then after that, I'm going on vacation for two weeks."

"Fantastic," Gerri replied. "Are you going skiing?"

Juliet's smile faltered a bit. "No, Raven talked me into going where the men are."

Gerri smirked at her "And where is that, dear?"

She couldn't help but roll her eyes. "The hot-as-hell beach."

Gerri chuckled. "I take it that's not a favorite place of yours?"

"Are you kidding me? I hate the sand. It gets everywhere and it's so hot. Give me a cold day in Alaska any day of the week."

"So, you wouldn't turn your nose up at a polar bear shifter?" Juliet stared at Gerri for a moment trying to determine if she was being serious or not.

"I would never turn my nose up at anyone,

honestly, but are you serious? You would set me up with a polar bear while I am in Alaska?" Juliet didn't know whether to be amazed, scared, or run like hell in the other direction.

"Maybe something a bit smaller would suit you," Gerri contemplated. "Promise me to keep an open mind while in Alaska and I will take care of the rest."

Juliet nodded. "If you set up Raven, Frost, and Ice, then I will trust you."

Gerri was about to reply, but Juliet's name was announced through the speaker system. "Where is Juliet?" Raven's mother was heading the single's auction on the stage up front. "Juliet Taylor, where are you? It's your turn, my dear."

Juliet groaned and tried to shrink into the wall. "There you are, way in the back." Everyone turned to find Juliet. Gerri laughed and gently pushed her forward. "Go, have an enjoyable date."

J uliet walked on stage and listened to Raven's mom read her biography. She tried to appear confident, but it wasn't every day a girl got paraded in front of a bunch of single people.

"Juliet is a geologist who travels the world with her job. She loves the outdoors and romantic settings with her partner. Our starting bid is $100."

Damn woman, *romantic settings with her partner*, sounded like she was trying to pimp her out now. And only $100 to start, she was a cheap date. Juliet tried not to laugh as she paraded around the stage and smiled at the audience.

She tuned out and didn't listen to the crowd or anything else Raven's mom said. She daydreamed instead about her trip to Alaska and then her dreaded beach trip. Moments later, she was drawn out of her thoughts when she heard sold. Juliet glanced over and saw a tall, really thin man standing there. She walked over and said hello.

"I understand you are going out of town for work shortly. Would it be to forward to ask you to accompany me for coffee tonight?"

Juliet looked at Raven's mom and then back to the gentleman standing in front of her. "I suppose we can do that. May I ask your name first?" He laughed and gestured for her to precede him down the steps. "My name is Theodore Grant. I thought we could get coffee to appease the rules of the auction and not interfere with your work. If you agree, we could meet again when you come home."

Juliet smiled at him. "Coffee would be lovely. There is a nice place down the street. I will follow you in my car." No way was she getting in a vehicle with a stranger, even if he did spend money on her. He was a bit formal. "I'll meet you there, I just want to say bye to some friends and let them know where I'm going." Theo nodded and left. Juliet watched him walk away and then turned to Raven's mom. "We are going to Corrie's diner down the street."

Raven's mom smiled and kept her bidding announcements going but she did wink at Juliet

The diner was close so it only took Juliet a couple minutes to get there. When she entered, Theodore was sitting at a table with two coffees in front of him. Shit! Was that sweet or creepy?

She walked over and sat across from him. "Thank you for bidding on me. That was really sweet. What do you do for work?"

He smiled. "I'm an accountant, but honestly, I am fascinated by you. Tell me about being a geologist. Gems are a hobby of mine. Being a geologist, you must be around a lot of rocks, right? Have you found gold on any of your expeditions?"

Juliet laughed. "No. Gold is sorta hard to find. You have to dig for it with big machines and mechanical sifting belts."

"Oh," Theo said, "it beats the old days. No panning in creeks for you?"

"Definitely!" Juliet replied. "All the big nuggets have been found. If we were back in the 1800s then maybe. They were many big deposits found back then. But nowadays, gold is just a commodity on the stock market."

"A very expensive commodity, if I believe correctly," Theo said, raising his brows.

"Yeah," Juliet answered, "last I looked, gold was selling at $38 per gram."

Theo thought about that for a second, his lips in a straight line and his brows drawn down in a slight frown. "How much is that a pound?

Juliet's focus turned inward. "There are around 450 grams to a pound, give or take, if I remember correctly. So that would be. . ." Juliet did the math in her head for 450 multiplied by $38 which happened to be a bit over— "A pound of gold would be around $17,100."

"Wouldn't it be great to have about a hundred pounds of that?" Theo chuckled at the response.

"That would be great," Juliet smiled at his remark, "but not happening in this lifetime. I'd be happy with a small cabin in the woods where you can't see your neighbors."

Theo shuddered. "No, thank you. I enjoy the city too much, I need the hustle and bustle. Too much quiet and I'd go stir crazy."

Juliet laughed but knew this was going nowhere. They had nothing in common and he was too interested in gold.

She glanced at her watch. "I'm sorry to cut this short but I do have a lot to do before I leave next week for Alaska. Do you mind if we call it a night?"

Theodore stood. "Of course not." He slid a business card out of his pocket and across the table. "Call me when you get back and we can get to know each other better."

Juliet took it and smiled. "Good night, Theodore. It was a pleasure to meet you."

THREE

"Tevrik," Frost said to him as he looked around the restaurant in Antler, Alaska, "having a mate is the best thing. You have no idea what you're missing."

Tevrik turned to his friend and cocked his head. "If I don't know what I'm missing, then I'm happier that way. Let it go." He really didn't want to hear how great having a mate was. Soon, his thinking would turn to jealousy and the dragon would smell it coming off his wolf in droves. Best to not entertain that fucking idea. He'd had such shitty luck finding his mate anyway.

"Come on, man," Frost smelled the sadness and anger coming from him and backed down.

Yes, Tevrik knew what his friend meant. But it didn't decrease the pain or memories of the past. And that incident was why Tevrik didn't consider himself worthy of having love. No, only strong, good alphas were allowed to be happy. He'd let people down. He didn't deserve happiness. Not anymore.

"You know," Frost said, looking down at his empty plate with food crumbs, "it was an accident. Someday you have to move on. You can't let what happened keep you from going forward."

"Yes, I can," he said a bit louder than he wanted. Eyes from nearby tables glanced at him. He wiped a hand down his face. "Look, Frost, thanks for trying to help me, but I don't need it. I'm happy where I am—"

"Away from your pack?" Frost said. "Wolves are not a solitary species, Tevrik—"

"This wolf is," he shot back. Rehashing the same conversation they had every time wasn't getting them anywhere. "Besides I have you and Ice when I want company. I don't want or need anyone else. I can even come into town."

Frost pulled out his phone and started typing. They sat quietly for a few seconds, Tevrik letting his emotions calm down. He'd let his anger come through and he knew Frost only wanted the best for him. He was a true friend. He blew out a breath. "Sorry, man."

Frost nodded, still typing on his phone. "It's fine. You know how Ice and I met Raven, right? Well, I just contacted her about setting you up." He tapped the phone screen and laid it on the table.

Tevrik drew his brows down. Was he kidding? "What do you mean? Why would you do that?"

Frost shrugged. "She actually contacted me first. I was just replying to her."

"No," Tevrik said immediately, "I will not go on a date with anyone. I don't need help."

Frost lifted his hands in front of himself. "Calm down, dude. I'm not asking you to." Tevrik eyed the phone turned down on the table and then glowered back at his soon-to-be ex-friend if some female with too heavy perfume and loaded with makeup walked in the door within ten minutes.

Marge approached the table, coffee pot in hand. "You guys want refills?"

Frost shook his head. "Nah, we're good," he said, glancing at Tevrik. Instead of going away, Marge stood there. After a few seconds, Tevrik looked up at her.

"How long has it been, Tev, since we saw you last?" she asked.

He sat back in his chair and rolled his eyes. "What

does it matter, Marge? I come into town when I need to get stuff."

She huffed. "Well, good thing you came in today. Make sure to get all your stuff before you leave. Snowstorm coming tomorrow. They said it was going to be a doozy for only being the start of November. You know we worry about you."

He did know that. "Yeah, thanks, Marge. I'll do that." She gave him a serious nod and walked away. What she didn't know was that he was prepared to survive the apocalypse if need be. Just because he lived secluded in the mountains didn't mean he was a fucking idiot. His wolf smelled the storm coming days ago when the air pressure began to drop. He'd figured out a thing or two during the past several winters.

Frost glanced at his watch. "Speaking of doing," his friend grinned at him and he smelled the beginnings of desire coming from him—fuck— "I'm meeting Ice and Raven at the house soon. Should probably stop at the general store on the way. We're out of chocolate frosting."

He smirked. "What? She bakes cakes all day for you?"

"No," Frost said. "Our mate likes to lick frosting off Frost." The dragon pointed to himself and waggled his brows. Tevrik was really going to puke up every bit of roast and potatoes he just ate. They tossed money on the table which included a nice tip for Marge and headed out.

A man at a table they past called to his friend. "Hey, Frost. You got a second?" Tevrik gave a nod indicating he'd wait outside.

The air in Antler was nippy, but it had been for several weeks. With a handful of hours of light, on its way down to a max of four hours in late December, the nights would only get longer and colder. Despite that, he wouldn't need a coat for a couple weeks. One great thing about his wolf, body heat was not a problem in Alaska.

As he stepped onto the asphalt parking lot around the back of the restaurant, he heard one of the voices that had kept him away from his wolf pack all these years.

"Well, look who it is, Petey," James Watson said. "Tevrik Awulf, wolf killer of the pack."

His wolf rankled, anger shooting in his veins, and Tevrik fought to calm him. These guys weren't worth his time. Petey and James were two idiots who hung out together when they were in school. James was the brains while Petey was the muscle. In fact, next to himself, Petey was the strongest kid. Though big, the boy never had the smarts to take down the alpha's kid.

He ignored them and continued toward his truck.

"Hey," Petey Mills said, "we're talking to you."

Tevrik ignored the jabs. His wolf wanted blood, but Tevrik knew that would only cause more drama. Shit, he was trying to avoid. He *wasn't* talking to them.

"He's leaving. Was it something we said?" one of the idiots mouthed off. "Don't ever come back to the pack. We don't want you there. Better off without you."

The other said, "I heard the pack leaders talking about getting a new alpha. Sure as shit, the son of the current alpha won't take over. He runs and hides. More of a failure than his alpha father."

Tevrik stopped. They could call him names and talk about him behind his back. But no one fucked with his family. No one.

He spun around and stalked toward the men. The fear in their eyes was short lived as they realized the odds were two against one. Didn't matter to Tevrik. He was taught an alpha keeps his cool and thinks before he reacts. He wanted their skin and blood on his claws. His self-pride might have been weak, but it wasn't nonexistent.

His father was the best alpha the pack had ever had. He'd brought them out of the stone age and into the modern century. They had strong, warm homes instead of drafty huts to live in. They had modern medical facilities they could go to instead of shamans who doctored according to myths and the "old" ways. They could depend on food always being available at the grocery. No one went hungry. The pack prospered more than ever before. How many past alphas could boast that?

"Oh, no," Petey chided, "wolf killer is pissed." The asshole shook his arms. "I'm so scared."

Well, he should've been. Tevrik marched up and swung so fast, it caught Petey off guard, tossing him flying. He landed a few feet away on his ass. James tried to attack when Tev was distracted, but when he threw a punch, Tevrik caught it with one hand.

When James popped out claws on his other hand, Tevrik's wolf pushed at his skin to get out, but this fight would be over before it really started. Before the dickhead could do anything, Tevrik squeezed the fist in his palm and twisted James around and slammed his chest against their truck.

James hollered from the pain. He always was a pansy. Tev whispered into his captive audience's ear, "Do not fuck with what belongs to me or those I care for. You will quickly find yourself pushing up daisies—"

Frost came around the corner of the building. "Hey!" he shouted. "What the hell is going on?" Tevrik released the asshole he smashed against the truck. "James Watson and Pete Mills? What the hell are you stupid fucks doing?"

Neither guy replied to Frost, just dashed for their pickup truck and tore out of the lot, a shovel falling from the back when they fishtailed onto the street.

Tevrik shook his head and hurried to the road to remove the lane hazard before an unexpecting driver hit it. Though he didn't have much to worry about. The shovel looked used enough to disintegrate on its own.

Frost stood behind him, looking at the tool. "Damn, I've never seen a shovel with the blade so bent and broken."

Tevrik tossed it into the trash container sitting in the corner. "That's typical for digging in the hills."

"Digging for what?" Frost asked.

He shrugged. "Who knows? Gemstones, gold, rocks?"

"Gold?" Frost grunted. "Seriously? They think they're going to find a gold mine?"

He shrugged again. "Knowing them, they're searching for the lost stash of Kitty Kalloway."

Frost stopped him with a hand on his chest. "Wait, what? Lost treasure? Do you believe that? If they were to find something, then what? You know they won't share it with the pack."

Tevrik laughed. The first time in a long time. "It's only a story, a myth that's not true."

"All myths are based on some truth, so tell me anyway," Frost said.

"All right." He took a moment to remember back to when he heard the story as a child. "Back in the Alaskan gold rush years, a hundred thousand men and women came to Alaska to find their riches. Most didn't, of course. But some did. One was a man named Kourvic Kalloway. He supposedly mined bags and bags of gold. A hundred pounds or something ridiculous."

Tevrik glanced at Frost to see if he was still following along. He had to admit that he occasionally missed talking with his friends. Living in the mountains could get lonely. He'd forgotten how fun it was to spend time with people like Frost and Ice.

"Kourvic knew how much his wife, Kitty, like to spend money, so he thought he'd be smart and hide all the gold, keeping a small amount with him for when

22

he wanted to buy something. Sneaking out to get more when he ran out. As usual, his wife got the truth out of him and when he refused to tell her where the hidden stash was, she killed him."

He waited for Frost to say something. After a moment of silence, the dragon raised a brow. "What? That's it?"

"Yeah," he answered. "Not much to it."

"Well, that's pretty damn lame for a gold legend, man," Frost said, frown on his face. Tevrik laughed.

Frost asked, "What happened to the wife? And why do those idiots think they can find the treasure with so little known about the couple?"

"I don't know," he shrugged. "It's just a moral story about hiding things from your mate. Maybe they found more information. James was always pretty damn smart."

At that second, Frost's phone chimed. He pulled it from his pocket and read the message he received. A wide smile grew on his face.

"What?" Tevrik asked. "And if it has anything to do with licking frosting, I do *not* want to hear about it."

"Nah, man," Frost replied. "This is from Gerri Wilder."

"Who?" Tevrik didn't remember that name, it wasn't anyone he knew.

"My friend I emailed when we were eating." Oh, right. Tevrik recalled that. "And she has answered, sorta, my request for help."

"Help?" he said. "Why didn't you ask me for help if you need it."

The dragon raised both brows. "The help is for you, wolf."

Tevrik didn't even want to know what this was about. He could only guess it involved a female, or several, who he wouldn't like, would find boring, and he'd have to suffer dinner with. Nope. Not happening. He headed toward his truck. "I'll catch you later—"

"No, wait. It's not what you think." Frost jogged up to him, handing him the phone. "Here, read for yourself."

Tevrik put his hands up. "I don't—"

"Read. It." Frost set the phone against his chest, pushing the plastic corner into his sternum.

"Fine." He snatched the device from his chest and looked at the screen.

Frost,

It's great to hear from you again. I hope all is well

with the both of you and Raven. You make such a lovely trio.

CONCERNING YOUR FRIEND TEVRIK AWULF, I have just the thing for him. Tell him to meditate on the subject of a mate in his usual spot. Who knows? Maybe love will fall right into his lap.

GIVE RAVEN a big hug for me.

LOVE ALWAYS,
   Gerri

TEVRIK HANDED THE PHONE BACK. "Love will fall right into my lap? Right." He shook his head. "You need to find better female friends, man."

"Believe it, dude. She matched us up with Raven, and she owns the Paranormal Dating Agency. Even a hermit like you had to have heard of it."

Shit! Of course, everyone had heard of the PDA. Hell, Frost and Ice mentioned using the agency to find a mate. He didn't need her help and he really didn't want it. All this mate talk was getting to him. "Look, Frost. Didn't you need to go *do* your mate?"

Frost gave him the biggest shit-eating grin, but Tevrik also saw the love for the dragon's mate in his eyes. "Yep, gotta go. Later."

With that, his friend stripped down and shifted into his dragon. Luckily, no one was looking. Did having a mate make one that reckless? He hoped not. Being reckless would get someone killed where he lived.

Tevrik hopped into his snowcat, pushing aside the supplies from the general store he purchased before lunch and started the two-hour trek to his mountain cabin.

FOUR

D amn, it was cold, and Juliet loved it. She stood next to her snow ATV and breathed in the fresh mountain air. Her co-workers thought she was crazy when she volunteered for the Book Mountain stat keeping duties. Who in their right mind wanted to hike up a mountain in subfreezing temperatures to record how deep a stick said the snow was, and any other experimentations? She would, but she wouldn't comment on the "right mind" part of the question.

This was the last task for the day. The one she loved the most—being on the highest peak just south of the Arctic Circle.

She closed her eyes and let the gentle wind brush

across her face, chilling her cheeks but making her feel alive. Her bright red snowsuit provided plenty of warmth to fight the coldness that could kill within minutes if exposed.

Overhead, a hawk screamed. She saw it corkscrewing in an air current not far from the peak. On occasion, she'd seen black bears, caribou, and mountain goats. And once, from a distance, she glanced at an elusive Canus Lupus Arcticus—the stunning snow-white arctic wolf.

She'd never forget that moment. The snowcat she'd rented for the journey up the mountainside stopped functioning halfway back to civilization after a routine stat count. Of course, there was no cell service in the middle of the tundra, so for all purposes, she was dead in the water. And she truly feared she would meet death soon. She couldn't walk in the elements for any length of time. It took over two hours to drive from town to the mountain range. On foot would take all day.

As she sat in the vehicle, her eyes roamed the vast brown landscape. She had to admit, the Alaskan tundra wasn't the prettiest place to die. But it was the place she'd want to be in her last hours. Where she felt the most at home, most in touch with nature and the earth.

Then in the far reaches of her eyesight, something moved. If it hadn't been for the white color against the dirt-colored ground, she might've never seen it. Her eyes tracked its movement from the edge of the woods across the frozen land toward her. She wanted to step outside the vehicle to get closer, but figured she'd frighten away whatever it was.

Instead, she remained in the snowcat, watching, breathless. When the creature stopped and turned sideways, lifting its nose into the air, Juliet recognized the animal as an arctic wolf. It was massive, the biggest wolf she'd ever seen. Freakily massive, actually. But still beautiful with its pure white, thick coat and deep-set eyes.

And she swore those eyes locked onto hers even though it was fifty yards away. In that magic moment, a part of her she didn't know existed came alive. Something primal and basic to life. Something she'd been missing until that moment. Her heart raced and lungs refused to take in air. What was happening to her?

Then, as if it was spooked, the wolf turned and tore across the ground, headed back toward the trees. A couple hours after that, a man from town who said he was just passing through hooked up the dead vehicle and towed her back in. She was fortunate that day. If not for the guy, she might've never seen her friends or family again.

After she'd returned home, that feeling of when she was with the wolf, the pure joy, calmness, openness, was gone and hadn't returned. She never figured out what happened that special moment, but it was the most spiritual thing ever to happen to her.

Now, staring over the mountain cliff to the valley below was the closest she'd come to that feeling. Most of the hills and creeks were dry and brown since the snow season hadn't started yet. Sure, the peaks always had snow, but thousands of feet below was permafrost.

And that reminded her she needed to get moving. A snowstorm was coming in tomorrow and the airport was closing early to prepare for it. If she didn't make it back in time, she'd miss her connecting flight to Aruba. The damn beach. Why did she let her best friend talk her into vacationing there? That's where the men were, but did she really want a man who was happy sitting on a beach?

Grabbing the binoculars and transmitting radio, she positioned herself in the usual spot where she could read the measurement of the snow-depth marker a hundred feet down the side of the incline. Propping her elbows on a boulder, she stared through the magnifying lenses and saw the stick marker had been pushed sideways into the snow.

Oh, come the fuck on. This was the second time that damn stick had fallen over in six months. Before she left NSIDC, a report came in about seismic activity in the Book Mountains. She didn't believe there could be movement on the range. The Book was the most northern part of the American Rockies and the continental plate was as solid as the ground in the Midwest.

Their equipment must've been malfunctioning. But now she wondered. With no animal prints in the snow around the pole, something knocked it over. It could've been the wind, but who knew? All it meant was that she'd have to go down and replant the stick. This trip wouldn't be as routine as she'd hoped.

She trudged back to the snow ATV and pulled out her climbing gear. Normally she enjoyed rock climbing—inside on a wall where hand and foot holds were placed in convenient spots and the rope was tied off on a five-inch metal beam. But this wasn't her first rodeo doing the real thing.

She slipped the harness up her legs, securing it around her padded snowsuit and attached the rope with all the carabiners and tools. After hooking into the rappelling device, she double checked all knots, carabiners, and the autoblock. This process always took so damn long, twice as long as it took to just rappel down the side. But safety first.

When Juliet reached the marker, she pulled it from the snow and moved a few feet to the side to find a better place to anchor it. She pushed the stick down, feeling for the surface, but the marker kept sinking and sinking. It was almost completely under the snow and it hadn't touched yet. "What the hell?"

She yanked it up and moved another foot over. Once again, the stick went down until the top was even with the snow. Getting frustrated, Juliet climbed a few feet and jabbed the pole through the snow to abruptly stop where it should. She recorded the number and transmitted it back to the lab with the note—*I'm officially on vacation now. See you in two weeks*.

Now she was puzzled and intrigued. Why did the stick not touch rock there like it did here? Only one solution: there was no rock there. It was either a very deep hole or a cave.

The Book Mountains were known for having extensive caving systems where water once eroded the rock to carve out long, winding tunnels. Could be that she found one? And if it was covered in snow, could it be no one has ever been in or even discovered it? Had she found a place on the planet where no person has ever tread? She would be the first in history to travel the rocky shaft?

With overwhelming excitement, Juliet dug away snow at the places her measurements couldn't be taken. She felt like a puppy digging its first hole to bury a bone. The snow went farther down than she'd thought it could. A huge pile was behind her when her fingers hit rock. She moved over a bit and kept digging, she continued to scoop out white powder until she found a hole. She'd reached it!

Carefully, she leaned forward to stick her head in. She smelled wet rock and dirt. It was a cave. She slipped her gloves off and pulled her phone from a pocket. Using the flashlight, she peeked inside. She screamed with joy when seeing the rock walls continuing back.

Juliet climbed inside and found she could stand. She was rather on the short side, so that didn't mean much to the size of the shaft. The rope pulled on her harness, keeping her from going any farther. Well, that wasn't happening. She unclipped and laid the rope on the snow. With giddiness she hadn't felt since her first kiss, she slowly moved into the space.

Several feet in, she saw primitive wall drawings similar to what Native Americans created in the

American southwest, but these showed two-legged figures wearing furs, or what she figured was fur. One section of art depicted many humans with spears chasing a big shaggy thing with four legs. Another portrayed spears sticking out of the big shaggy thing lying on the ground. So she wasn't the first person to discover the cave, but this was still fascinating.

While scanning the walls, her foot bumped against something that caused a loud avalanche of noise. The light revealed an old wooden box and several burlap bags with their tops closed with wire. Her foot had hit a dilapidated shovel that fell onto metal pie-pan looking items.

Crouching, she dug through the pile and realized this equipment was old enough to be used during the goldrush well over a hundred years ago. Along with shallow pans, picks, and empty bags were a couple wood boxes with screen-like material for the bottom. That was an iconic sifting box for panning in a creek. All these things were for digging and sifting for rocks.

A thought crossed her mind and she turned to the small closed chest. The leather strap wrapping the container had disintegrated in places. The rough-hewn metal buckle hung by a thread. When she touched the clip, it fell to the ground creating a poof of dust.

Gently, Juliet's shaking fingers lifted the lid and was greeted with a brilliance only gold made. Ohmygod, ohmygod, ohmygod. She could barely breathe.

The heavy top slipped from her fingers and slammed down, crumbling to wooden shards on the nuggets. Oh, shit. She jerked her arms back, not wanting to touch it again and make the whole thing fall apart. Instead, she turned to the side and poked one of the burlap bags. Her finger went through the rotting material making an exit for the golden contents to flow out. Shit. Shit. Shit.

She sat back against a cold damp wall and stared at the treasure. This was crazy. Stuff like this never happened to her. Was she dreaming? Holy hell. She wondered how it got here and why it was still here. If a miner from the goldrush era hid it here, why didn't he come back for it? He more than likely died. This land wasn't for the weak.

What should she do with it? She couldn't carry it out easily with no containers, and it would be heavy! There had to be fifty or sixty pounds at least sitting there. She would have to come back and get it out without alerting anyone else. Damn, that was a million dollars!

People would kill for this find. She had to be careful how she handled this. She couldn't walk into the bank and yell she found gold, who would help her carry it. Good way to get kidnapped again. But she'd be rich beyond belief. She could build her dream cabin on ten acres of land and live the rest of her life doing what she wanted.

Then another thought hit her, what if this stash was fake? She scooped up a small handful and inspected it close up. It looked real, but only testing in a lab would verify. She'd send these to her lab before she left for Aruba. Hopefully, everyone was trustworthy at the lab and wouldn't snoop and figure out where she found these nuggets. It was a chance she would have to take. With luck she'd have an answer when she got back. Holy crap, if this was real... how had no one else ever stumbled on this treasure trove? How did she get so lucky?

She was tucking the nuggets in an interior pocket of her snowsuit when a strange vibration rolled through her back and butt. Dust fell from the ceiling of the cave. The vibes became stronger to shake the ground. Holy fuck, was this the seismic activity she didn't think real? Hallelujah, praise the powers that be! She was a believer now, no time to panic though. She had to get out, she didn't want to be buried underground! She would never be able to do anything with the gold!

Juliet sprang to her feet and rushed to the front of the cave, panic filled her body and she found herself gasping for air as she rushed toward the hole. When reaching the entrance, a different kind of rumble, not as deep as before, traveled up her feet and legs. As she crawled through the snowy tunnel, she grabbed onto the rope to link to her harness as soon as she reached the surface.

The sunlight ahead was a welcome sight even if the second rumble hadn't stopped yet, she felt like crying in relief. The sun hitting her face was a wonderful feeling, now she stood a chance of surviving. She twisted around to get her feet out first, and when she stood to clip the carabiner to her harness, a wall of snow smacked her in the chest, sweeping her down with the rest of the avalanche.

FIVE

Tevrik took a deep breath of the musty, earthy air inside the cavern. It had been a while since he'd visited here. He wasn't sure if that was good or bad. Being cradled in Mother Earth like this soothed his anxious wolf and calmed his restless soul.

Thirteen years ago, this place had been a godsend. He'd wandered the wilderness, lost and away from his family, his pack. He could never go back. He'd allowed the unthinkable to happen and his life would no longer be the same. His future of taking his father's position of alpha when he retired turned into a pipe dream. No one would want him to lead them. No one would trust him with their life. Rightfully so.

Cold, bitter, and hungry, he'd stumbled onto the

cave accidentally. His younger self nestled inside, out of the wind and falling snow. His wolf smelled food skittering around in crevices and behind boulders. It took some patience, but his wolf was able to catch enough rodents to stop the pain in his belly.

While he waited for the storm to pass, he trekked through the winding rock pathways, sometimes crawling on his stomach in inches-high openings between stone walls, sometimes turning sideways and sucking in his gut to get through cracks.

By the end, he'd traveled for hours through the twists and turns coming to the opening in the cave ceiling that in his mind was now sacred. This was where he vowed to himself, he would be a changed man. No longer would he be the teenager, so full of himself with no idea how the real world worked. Careless and ignorant.

He believed Mother Earth saved his unworthy ass that night, leading him to this place. She gave him shelter when he was homeless, offered him food when he was hungry, and comforted his soul when he was in torment. He promised to listen to her and learn to live by her rules. Only out of her hand would he survive.

Over the years, Tevrik dug a path, chipping away rock by rock, that allowed an easier journey through the treacherous terrain. That first time he lifted himself to peek out the opening over the ledge, he was amazed how up the mountain he had come.

Starting at the base of the incline, the excursion took him several hundred feet up through the mountain's belly.

As he approached the location now, so many years later, the trail worn by his tread, by his hands gliding over the same rock time after time, he stopped and gazed at the sight.

A ramp split from the main tunnel, giving him an upward path along the wall to a flat ledge several feet higher than the floor of the main passage. Above that leveled rock was the three-foot gap in the ceiling. Through that elongated hole, soft light poured in like the sun's rays shining down from behind a large cloud. If an angel came out of that light, it would not surprise him.

He sat in his usual spot under the gap with his back to the wall, the opening directly overhead. Sometimes he built a small fire if a chill had set in, but with the bright sun today, that wasn't needed.

He reminded himself he wasn't here because some woman in a city said he should meditate about a mate in his usual place. No. Not completely, anyway. He was here to settle the guilt in his subconscious. It had been many years since anyone had openly accused him of being a wolf killer. Fucking James and Petey.

All the memories he'd managed to suppress were back full force and he couldn't go through those again. He hoped this magical place would once again provide him with the peace he needed.

With a deep breath, he took in the scents of the wilderness around and above him—the cave, snow, fresh air, small creatures rummaging for food on the slope, burnt wood from his previous campfires. The breath out took with it the toxic thoughts and emotions that beat and cut into him. Let it go.

For some reason, that damn message Frost showed him from the woman popped into his head. She thought she was being funny when saying his mate would fall into his lap. What a stupid thing to say to someone who wasn't worthy of such happiness. Another breath in. Toxic out. He'd survived this long without a mate. He could go on the same way. Mother Earth would provide.

Suddenly, his body tingled. At first, he thought the vibration he felt was from a large animal running down the mountainside nearby, but he ruled that out when the rock around him shifted. That was an earthquake. There had been a few of those this past year.

Then he heard a sound that shocked him immobile for a moment. It couldn't be. Could it? The crack and boom of a snow layer breaking free from the surface. Avalanche.

Tevrik remained where he was. He was safe from the onslaught even with the gouge in the rock overhead. The snow would be moving too fast to fall inside. Some spray or small rocks on the bottom of the pile might drift in, something heavy enough for gravity to immediately take hold of and bring down. But that was it. Whenever the rumbling stopped, he'd make his way back to his cabin.

He watched as wisps of flying snow passed by. He knew when the mass of snow plowed over, the cave would become pitch black. As he readied his flashlight, a bright red color above grabbed his attention. As the snow covered the gap, the red mass fell through the hole, right into his lap.

Luckily his animal reflexes were sharp and fast. He caught the thing before it landed on him. But now sitting in the absolute dark, he had no idea what he held. The flashlight had been knocked out of his hand when he reached up, so that was useless. All he smelled was dirt and snow. He'd have to use his sense of touch.

The bulky thing was longish like a tree, but trees

were not wrapped in red. Plus it wasn't stiff like a trunk. It bent when he caught it.

The outer covering was some kind of plastic material that made a rasping sound when he rubbed his hand over it. Most of it felt covered in snow so he brushed away what he could. But that didn't help any. He squeezed on the material finding it fluffy for several inches before hitting something solid.

This was ridiculous. He was never good at guessing games. He needed to find his damn flashlight. Leaning to the side, he sniffed for the acidic smell of the batteries and found it not too far away. He switched it on and looked at the red and snow-hidden balled up mass.

He pulled on the top of the red material and it rolled over. In the process, he saw a flash of a human hand. Oh shit. This was a human. Yes, now he smelled blood. The snow and clothing had blocked any scent.

He moved toward the head of the body which was tucked into the hood of the coat. Snow was packed in also. He must've been hit hard from the front for that to happen. Which probably meant internal injuries and possible concussion. If the dude was even alive.

As quickly and carefully as he could to avoid making the injuries worse, Tevrik pulled the hood off, letting the snow fall away, exposing the face. . .of an angel.

Her delicate jawline and high cheekbones were under a mess of mud, blood, and snow. Her lips were an unhealthy tinge of blue.

He checked for a pulse on her neck since he couldn't hear her heartbeat over the noise of the avalanche. It was there, but weak and a bit erratic. She needed to be warmed immediately. But if he lifted her, he could hurt her more. There was no way an ambulance with a stretcher could get up here. He either carried her or she died here on the cold rock. Put that way, the choice was obvious.

Putting his flashlight in his mouth, he used both hands to pick her up and hold her close to his body. The snowsuit she wore wouldn't allow any of his body heat to reach her, but hopefully that meant enough of her own body heat was retained to keep her from hypothermia. He'd find out when they got back to the cabin.

He could smell very little of her natural scent. When a human body was cold, the extremities were the first to freeze as the bodily functions focused on keeping the core warm. But with the little he could smell, he could tell she was human and not a shifter. That made her chances of surviving much less.

Humans were so damn fragile. Their bones snapped like twigs and their skin was practically useless against anything sharp. They bled so easily.

After several minutes of hiking downhill through the cave, Tevrik kicked open his cabin's door and carried his load into the warm room. He laid her on the bed then stood back and looked at her in the light of day.

She was even more stunning than before. Instead of an angel walking from the sun rays, she fell from the heavens right into his lap. It was the most ridiculous yet accurate description he could come up with. He sounded like a fucking pussy but the most beautiful woman he'd ever seen had just fallen on him from heaven. Shit, he needed a drink.

He blew out a breath, thinking where to start with warming her body. He unbuttoned and unzipped the heavy overcoat then slipped it off her arms and from under her back. The overall-style snow pants came above her waist and hooked over her shoulders. Smart outfit. It was the best design to keep snow away from the body in just about any condition.

When he draped the coat over the back of a chair close to the fire, he saw the letters NSIDC in white stitch. He had no clue what that stood for. With that many letters, it had to be something important. Somebody would be missing her right away.

He leaned down to the fire and rotated out a rod holding a large black pot over hot coals. He dipped a hand towel into the iron kettle to see how hot the water was. Burning his fingers, he got his answer. Stupid. He scooped a handful of snow from outside and dumped it into the pot. After stirring, the water became a pleasant temperature.

With the wet cloth, he gently dabbed at the woman's face, wiping away the dirt and blood that had dried to her delicate flesh. Her skin was flawless except for several faded freckles across her nose which made her even cuter. His little pixie.

Her scent wafted to him and his wolf whispered *mine*. How the fuck? No. That matchmaker couldn't have known, could she? His mate fell into his lap. Why did he go to the cave? He didn't deserve to find her. He didn't deserve to be happy.

That dark place inside him crept up. The place that told him he was worthless. He pushed the darkness down. That wasn't a place he wanted to be in again. Besides, he needed to get this, his, woman back to town in a few hours. The snow would arrive a bit earlier than he originally thought. Not tomorrow, but tonight.

Focus returning to his patient, he noted bruising already on her face. She was going to be very sore tomorrow. He glanced down at her poofy overalls. They were good protection from the weather, but how much of a cushion did they give for broken bones. Shit. One of her legs could've broken off and he wouldn't have noticed.

He ran his hands over her arms to make sure nothing was misaligned. Her green thermal shirt clung to her arms, making detection easy. But the pants were another story. He'd have to take them off to check her legs.

After he removed her boots—she'd tied the damn things with double knots which after ten minutes of trying to get them undone, he was tempted to pop out a claw and slice the damn things—he unhooked the straps from her shoulders and worked the overalls down her body. When he reached her waist, he paused.

Surely she had thermals or jeans on underneath, right? Shit, he felt like a pervert undressing an unconscious woman. Yeah, had her in the house for ten minutes and had her clothes off already. He shook his head.

He inched the snow pants lower to see the waistband of a pair of jeans. He blew out a breath and slid the red fabric completely off and draped them over the footboard. Carefully, he smoothed his hands down each leg feeling for bumps under the muscle. And muscles she had. She was strong and toned like she ran or hiked a lot. He imagined her legs bare, wrapped around his waist, their silkiness, shapeliness, her skin so soft as he fucked her.

A sudden heat struck him, sweat beading on his upper lip. He shoved away from the bed and left the curtained-off area. He was too close to the fireplace beside the bed. Yeah, that was it—the fire was too hot. Denial, he knew it well. She wasn't really his mate; he wasn't attracted to her. He wasn't thinking about waking her and warming her skin to skin. Sliding his cock into her warmth and taking her hard and fast.

He grabbed a metal cup from the cabinet and dipped it into the water cauldron and lifted out a full mug of hot water. Tevrik carried it with him out the side door into the room he grew veggies and fruits in. Stopping at the herbs, he plucked a touch of chamomile, ginger, and lemongrass and placed them in the center of a square piece of fabric that he gathered and tied at the top with a string.

From there, he dropped the herb packet into the water to steep. At least she could have tea when she woke. Not much more he could offer, well, his body but not his heart. This too would pass and he could get back to his day-to-day life.

And wasn't that damn pathetic? He had nothing more he could offer to anyone, much less a mate. No woman in her right mind would want to stay here in a cabin he built with his own hands in an environment that could kill the mightiest of shifters. No, his wolf would have to deal with her leaving. She couldn't be theirs.

Tevrik turned back to the bedroom where the woman laid. He hesitated, then pushed aside the muslin curtain separating the bedroom from the living area. He set the mug on the bedside table, trying not to look at her. Just her presence made him anxious.

Damn, she looked so fragile. His protective instincts ignited with a fury. Something he hadn't felt since he was with the pack. She was perfect, a porcelain doll and he was taking her down the mountain as soon as she woke.

With shaky hands, Tevrik grabbed her coat from the chair by the fire and draped it over her body. The heat trapped in the material would keep her warm for a while. Long enough for him to get control of himself.

His wolf growled, he didn't want their mate to

leave. Tevrik struggled to contain him. He backed away from the bed and the angel in it. He was not going to claim his mate, not caress her body from head to toe, slide his cock into her warm pussy over and over until she begged for more. He struggled against the temptation she posed, and it ate at him.

In the living room, he rapidly paced in front of the fire, his hands pulled at his hair. What the hell was happening to him? He sees a beautiful woman and he and his wolf fucking freak out?

In his T-shirt and jeans, he stomped outside and saw the wood chopping station. Yes, he needed more wood before the storm hit. Not really, but that's what he told himself as he hefted the ax and swung, splitting a large piece with one blow. And then another and another.

SIX

Arhythmic sound, like a drum with an intermittent beat, woke Juliet. She tried to place the noise, but none of her neighbors had a bass drum. Maybe one of the kids took up marching band.

Then she smelled burning wood and heard popping and crackling like a campfire would make. Her first thought was that her condo was on fire. She bolted up, eyes wide, and pain so intense hit her in the chest, she almost blacked out. She fell back onto the bed and she didn't move, didn't breathe, she hurt so bad.

Eventually, she had to breathe a little. Just a little, not enough to cause agony. Eyes opening again, she stared at a ceiling that was not in her home. She was somewhere else. Someone had kidnapped her again? Terror from her abduction by Antler's sheriff earlier in the year rushed through her. She had to get away.

Then her brain registered that her arms were free as were her feet. Whoever had captured her was really dumb not to bind her. Then again, maybe she wasn't in danger. She thought back to her last memory which was sending the snow depth stat to the lab with a note she'd be back in two weeks. Nothing after that.

One thing was for certain. She wasn't on the beach. But where was she?

Her eyes trailed down the side of the shaved-log wall, a window close to the end of the bed. She started to reach out to touch it to see if it was real wood, but her ribs twinged with pain. She rolled her head to see the other side of her bed. That wall consisted of stacked rocks of various sizes.

In the spaces between the rocks were gaps she could see the fire. Heat filtered through the holes keeping the area she was in warm. She knew the rocks would be warm too, giving off heat to hold the temp steady for several hours if the fire went out. Smart use of natural materials to stay warm.

The thumping sound continued. The source was outside, not too far. Tilting her head toward her toes, she saw a curtain draped over a whittled-smooth tree limb that reached from wall to fireplace wall, not that the distance was that much. Only the bed and a small table next to her pillow occupied the space. Couldn't be more than seven-foot square.

She glanced at the piece of furniture beside her and for a moment she was stunned by its beauty. A painstaking, hard-carved image of wolves along a creek in the forest—oh my god, done in relief even —was whittled into the top. The trees looked to be swaying in the breeze and the creek had fish that looked like they were underwater. How was this made? Had to be with a computer and fine pointed tools. This must've cost the owner a fortune. Though you wouldn't know it by everything else in the place.

A dented metal cup sat on the detailed table. She'd love to have a drink of water. Maybe if she slowly sat up, she'd be okay. Using her arms, she carefully lifted her shoulders and pushed back, keeping her stomach muscles relaxed. She scooted up a foot before pain sucked her breath away, constricting her chest and lungs.

After the pain relinquished, she was able to reach the cup and drag it closer. Taking it into her hands, she smelled sweet, calming herbs. Chamomile for certain. She sipped—ginger and lemongrass. The temperature was perfect for hot tea. The liquid felt good going down.

What else was there to see? The thumping beat on.

Beyond the partially opened curtain at the end of the bed, she saw the front wall with a window letting in deep red light. Was the sun setting? She had a couple hours before sunset, if she remembered correctly.

Below the window was a table for two with only one chair. Both looked handmade from real trees. She imagined the reliefs decorating the table were astounding.

That was all of the cabin she could see. Her tiny bedroom was tucked into a back corner next to the fireplace wall.

Cozy, she kinda liked it. She thought about all the crap in her bedroom at home. Everything was just material objects to look at. She didn't *need* any of it. Just a bed and a small table.

Setting the half-full cup on the table, she felt much better. She had control of her situation and was ready to meet the home's owner.

"Hello?" The sound scratched out barely a whisper. She could try taking a deeper breath, but the idea of pain radiating through her wasn't pleasing. Now that she was sitting up, she pegged the thumping sound at a short distance on the other side of the wall next to her. If she could get to the window a few feet away, she could see what the hell was making that noise.

Very slowly and carefully, she inched her way toward the glass. Trying to ignore the jabs of pains, she leaned to peek out.

Holy hunk with an ax.

A tall, hunk of a man stood thirty feet away murdering chunks of wood. The ax swung up, lifting his white shirt which was drenched in sweat and clung to his chest. Talk about a wet T-shirt contest. Ripples all the way down his abs, she drooled at the sight.

His biceps bulged, stretching the short sleeves' cuffs. Muscles in his forearms were even pumped. The worn jeans he sported were tight around the thighs, and when the ax fell, he leaned forward showing her his very rounded, very bitable ass.

Her nose bumped against the glass. Was she actually drooling? Damn, her panties were probably wet.

As if he heard her thoughts, he turned and looked directly in the window. She sprang back from the sill, sending knife jabs through her sides. Her body contorted, hitting her head against the footboard and rolling to drop onto the floor. She heard a pop and prayed it wasn't a rib bone breaking.

Juliet lay on the hardwood, not breathing, not blinking, not anything but feeling the piercing fire shooting through her torso and head. She felt her body convulse and thankfully passed out.

Coming to, her first thought was what was licking her face. The second thought was had the licker ever brushed their teeth. Massive dog breath. When a high-pitched whine met her ears, she opened her eyes to see a panting muzzle below a pair of penetrating sapphire eyes. Fully white and fluffy, the dog was beautiful and cute with his tongue hanging out.

The dog got to its feet and Juliet saw how big it was. She was wrong; it wasn't a dog, but a wolf—huge Arctic wolf. A lot like the one she saw a long time ago.

But blue eyes weren't characteristic for an arctic wolf. From her research on the animal, she learned they had brown eyes. So what was she looking at?

Considering she had dog slobber on her face and no tooth marks, she figured the wolf was tame. Must've been the guy's pet. She could give him an earful about domesticating wild animals. She said out loud to the wolf,

"While having a wild pet might be nice for the

human, it's not the best for you. You can't follow your natural instincts if kept in a house. And if that man chains you to keep from running away, I will eviscerate him." Anger flared then died. She was talking to an animal like it would reply. Maybe she hit her head when her ribs were hurt.

Shaking her head at her insaneness, she realized she needed to get off the damn floor. When she took a bigger breath to sit up, pain speared her side, stealing the air from her lungs. The ache was so sharp, it brought tears to her eyes. She lay flat, not moving, breathing as little as possible.

The puppy, well, big wolf puppy, whimpered and settle on the floor next to her, licking her cheek. Whining, he rested his head on the wood beams. If she didn't know better, she'd swear the wolf understood the pain she was in. Maybe animals could. She never had a dog.

Sweat popped out on her brow. How that could happen in this cold atmosphere was beyond her, but her body wasn't doing well at the moment. The animal scooted closer and dug his nose under her hand. Juliet lifted her fingers and scratched under the furry chin. So soft. She'd never felt fabric this luxurious. Showed Mother Nature couldn't be outdone with fake human crap.

"Okay, puppy, we've got to get back into bed or freeze on this damn floor. Where is your owner? I know he saw me through the window. Why hasn't he come in?" Her voice was barely above a whisper as she tried not to breathe much.

She might not be able to move her upper body, but her legs were fine. Bending her knees, she planted her feet and pushed. Her top wasn't slick material, but she slid at least a foot. With her head finally at the small table next to her pillow, she wondered how she was getting way up on the mattress.

Her bangs were drenched with sweat as was her sleeve from dabbing at her forehead. Since when was pushing five feet across the floor hard work? Apparently when ribs were broken.

Shit. She rolled her head toward the wolf intently watching her. One thing she knew—if the man had a sweet, loving pet, then he wasn't a mean person. He was probably even "safe."

"Seriously, where is your owner? He may be drop-dead gorgeous, having abs with more peaks and valleys than the Book Mountains. And an ass that would squeeze nicely in my hands. Not to mention—"

Whining, the wolf put its paws over its eyes. It was so damn cute, she barked out a laugh and passed out from the pain and exhaustion.

SEVEN

The steady rhythm of setting a piece of wood on the stump, swinging the ax, slicing the chunk, picking up another piece, swinging the ax, slicing the chunk, calmed Tevrik. Out in the cold a few steps from his cabin, his heart pounding, blood rushing through his veins, and the breeze on his face, made him feel alive. A lot of times as he lay in Mother Earth's domain, it was so silent, so dark, he wondered if he could be dead.

But no. Simply dying would be too easy for him. He needed to endure the pain and loneliness for a long time to atone for his misdeeds.

He set another log on the stump, swung the ax, sliced the chunk.

She couldn't be his mate, well, she could, but she would remain unclaimed. He didn't deserve happiness. Not now. Never. This was a mean joke. Fate had delivered his angel, so he'd suffer more when she went away. Given him a taste of what he would've had if he hadn't fucked up so badly.

Fuck. Already he felt the mating call wanting to connect, stretching for the one person born to be his. He couldn't let that happen. He would take her into town when she woke. His wolf rocketed up, snarling, biting, scratching to get out. *Mine*.

Movement out of the corner of his eye caught his attention, she was awake. He turned to look in the window and glimpsed an image of blond hair before it disappeared.

His wolf took him to his knees. He wanted to shift and be close to her. His clothes tearing into shreds, Tevrik ceded to the wolf. He had no choice. He gave a full-body shake, took a deep breath, scenting things it hadn't in years. One smell was the pain from his mate. In this form, maybe he could resist the mating pull.

He ran to the front of the cabin and pushed on the door until it opened. His mate lay on the floor beside the bed. He hurried inside and sniffed her. Fuck, she smelled so good, he licked her cheek, hoping to wake her. Her heartbeat was strong. She was in no danger of dying.

Her nose wrinkled up and Tevrik realized he was breathing dog breath right into her face. He backed up and lay on the floor. He didn't want to frighten her when she woke. If he looked harmless and cute, maybe she wouldn't freak out with a wild animal in the house.

He whined, and her eyes opened, staring directly into his. At that moment, he felt their connection click. They were mates, and nothing could be done about it. She stared at him for a long time. He wondered what went through her head.

Her head turned, and she took a deep breath and started to sit up. The scent of intense physical torment filled the air. She fell back. He crawled closer and licked her cheek again. That was all he could do in this form. He couldn't trust himself in human form, the pull was too strong. As his wolf, he could stay by her side and give her comfort.

He wanted to take away her pain. She barely breathed. What was wrong with her? What was hurting so much? Shifters healed when they shifted so he could only imagine what she was going through. He whined with dismay. How could he comfort her?

She scratched under his chin and he about died, it

felt so good. Damn, he'd forgotten how wonderful it was to be scratched and petted.

The woman spoke, barely a whisper. Her breathing was still shallow. Maybe her ribs were injured. That was very likely for being in an avalanche. Wait. Did she ask about his owner? *Owner*, my ass, the wolf thought.

His mate bent her legs and pushed herself along the floor. She was smart and resourceful, but it was still painful for her. That sour scent followed. He watched, staying close, crawling with her as she moved. He was an asshole, he should have shifted and helped her. Not let her suffer by moving her body. Reaching as far as she could go, she started talking again. This time, the smell from her was fucking delicious. The smell of arousal, she was talking about him chopping wood. Even injured, she was thinking about being attracted to him.

Uh—oh. Abs like mountains, and an ass she could squeeze. If he could blush in wolf form, he would be beet red. He put his head down and tried to cover his ears, but only got to his eyes with his paw.

She let out a laugh and then a moan. Then she lay quiet, not moving. She was injured badly. He picked up her steady pulse and released the breath he held.

There was nothing he could do as a wolf. He had to shift and control his need for her. Her voice was an aphrodisiac, and he wanted to feel her touch on his skin, not just his wolf's fur.

He shifted and looked down at his mate unconscious before him. Probably a good thing, his being naked might have scared her. Carefully, he placed his hands alongside her breasts and let his hands roam along the bones under his fingers. Slowly, he slid down her sides, feeling for broken or misaligned ribs.

Nothing was out of place at least, but he felt large, tight knots. Could be a cracked rib or just deeply bruised bones making the muscles squeeze around her lungs constricting her breathing. He could take care of that. As far as he could tell, she wasn't in physical danger. Which was a miracle in itself. He'd seen plenty of avalanches and had no desire to ride one down the mountain.

There was little choice in how to get her back into bed. He'd have to lift her. This time, he pulled the covers back, then put a hand between her shoulder blades and slid the other under her ass. He couldn't help but notice how full and soft it felt. He wondered how she would feel with him slapping against her ass as he pumped in and out of her.

Fuck. He was disgusted with himself. Here she was in pain and his cock was so hard he could drive nails. He lifted her into the bed then covered her properly. For a moment, he stared down at her. She was perfect, beautiful. She was his. No, she wouldn't ever be his for the taking. She was someone passing through. He would deny himself his mate.

He straightened, anger taking him. He wanted to rail against the world, tear into fate, for this cosmic prank. Giving her to him then taking her back, but it was up to him to send her away so there was no one else to blame.

From a wooden trunk on the other side of the curtained area, he took out clothes and dressed, then sat by the fireplace. He left the bedroom curtain pulled to the side so he could see her where she was passed out. What was he going to do? What if he did keep her? Would that be so bad? He'd not think about the small issue of having her permission. Who was he kidding? He'd never do that to any human or animal.

To keep her, he'd have to persuade her to stay. He looked around his pathetic hovel. Again, who was he kidding? No female in her right mind would want to stay here. First off, it was always colder than a witch's tit. Women liked the sun and beach. There was nothing around but snow and the woods. No pizza delivery. Amazon did not drop packages at the front door. And going out to eat meant hiking for caribou, then killing, skinning, and cutting it up.

He was so fucked. The only way he'd keep his mate would be to move back to the pack. Snowball's chance in hell of that happening. He didn't want a pack and they didn't want him.

Movement on the bed caught his eye. She was waking. He stayed where he was, not wanting to scare her. Her eyes opened then immediately met his. His pulse raced. He could hardly breathe. His wolf howled in his head. She was more beautiful than he thought.

Her eyes widened, seeing him, but she remained calm. Her tongue peeked out and swiped her lips. Goddamn, he almost came on the spot. He needed to pull his shit together. *Mate.*

He asked, "Would you like a cup of tea?"

When she smiled, her face lit up to rival heaven. He pointed to the drink on the small table beside her. "I'm going to get your cup."

She nodded.

His eyes wouldn't leave hers. He tried to get up, but his legs didn't work. He'd have to get closer to her. Damn, how he wanted to be near her, but the temptation was too much. Be near her body that was, thankfully, hidden under blankets. When he hadn't moved, her brows drew down. Oh shit. She had to be wondering what the hell was wrong with him.

He popped up, knocking over the stool he sat on. When he bent over to pick it up, his foot stepped on the fireplace ash rake and the handle flew up and smacked him in the leg. That startled him enough that he straightened and hit his head on a wall shelf, a small whittled wolf fell to the floor. He decided to leave it there as he rubbed his head.

Could he look any more like a total idiot? What were the odds that she didn't see any of that? He glanced at her to see her jaw dangling and eyes shining with humor. Dammit, she saw it all. Locating the cup, he dashed in, grabbed it, and rushed out, not looking at her.

From the herb garden, in addition to the regular tea spices, he added willow bark to help the pain from bouncing around in the snowcat when he drove her back into town. He packaged the herbs to let them steep while he mixed in the ground bark. He walked back, carrying the tea.

Without incident, he set the cup beside her. Then

he looked at her prone on the bed, unable to sit up. Then he looked back to the cup. How was she going to drink it?

"I don't think you have any broken ribs, so I can try to pull you closer to the headboard to prop you up enough to sip from the cup. Would that be all right?" She whispered a yes. Great. Now he had to figure out how to move her without touching her. That would be a problem. He stretched his arms toward her but stopped before his hands made contact. He pulled back and thought about using the sheet as a buffer. Then he realized how much of a dumbass he was being.

Just because he touched her didn't mean he would fall madly in love with her. Fuck, you'd think by the way he was acting, he hadn't been around women in a long time. It had been years since he'd had sex, but he saw women anytime he went into town.

He lifted her, hands in her armpits, and scooted her back. She sucked her lips in, biting down to keep from yelling with the pain he assumed. But soon enough, she was settled with her shoulders propped up. He handed her the tea and she sipped, relaxing a bit afterward.

He felt stupid standing there with his thumb up his

ass watching her luscious lips as they puckered for the sip, and her throat glide up and down as she swallowed. He could imagine her sucking on his cock, her lips wrapped around him, swallowing as he came in her mouth. He cleared his throat and stepped away from the bed.

Maybe she was hungry? Not that he was looking for an excuse to prolong her stay in his house, but he couldn't let her leave until the tea helped with her pain. From a timber box, he pulled out a carved wooden plate. From different containers, he pulled dried fruits slices—apple, orange, and mango. There weren't any bananas left. Those were his favorite.

On the other side of the fire from the water kettle, the griddle sizzled. He rotated it out and took green beans, corn on the cob, and fried sliced tomatoes and put them on the plate. And shit. He dug around for silverware. Normally he ate with his hands. Most of his food was finger ready.

After the dish was filled, he carried it around the corner to her. Her eyes popped open wide when she saw what he held. Her brows drew together.

"Wow," she whispered, "my stomach isn't that big."

He felt his face warm, and not from the fire. "I, uh, well," shit, he sounded smart, "I'll eat what you don't." Then he cringed. He remembered his mother always getting on him for eating off his sibling's plates, as they ate off his. Fuck, he must seem like a heathen to her. City girl lost in the wilderness with a caveman. Well, wolfman.

"Works for me," she whispered. He stared at her a moment to make sure she said what he thought she did. His mate didn't mind sharing her food with him. He handed her the plate and dragged a stool next to the bed.

She picked up the dried fruit and popped chunks into her mouth. "This is good. Did you make this?"

"Yeah, these are from a batch I picked earlier in the year," he replied.

"You picked these yourself?" He nodded to her question. "I didn't think Alaska had fruit trees."

"It doesn't," he answered. He smiled at her confusion. "I'm able to grow just about anything in the greenhouse."

She looked at the plate then looked up at him. "Did you grow all of this?" Once again, he nodded. "No grocery store?"

He laughed at that. "No. The general store is a two-hour drive and it doesn't have all that much."

She held out a peach slice for him. He took it and ate it. "Thank you." Her voice was getting softer as

69

she worked to breathe and chew and talk. "My name is Juliet Taylor."

He startled a bit. He hadn't even thought to get her name or give his. Duh. He was an idiot who'd lived in isolation too long.

"I'm Tevrik Awulf." He held his hand out and she smiled, shaking his hand. Her skin was warm and silky. He wanted to slide his hand up her arm and onto her shoulders and down—he cleared his throat. "Nice to meet you, Juliet."

She handed him a green bean. "I haven't heard either of those names before. Are they family names?"

"Yes. Tevrik means little wolf and the last name means mighty wolf."

"Your family must like wolves," Juliet replied. Tevrik froze. Shit. Double shit. Humans knew of shifters and lived side by side with them but most didn't realize who they were. Would she freak out if she figured out what he was? For generations, his pack kept itself isolated from humans. But as Alaska became more populated, their main source of meat— moose and caribou—declined rapidly as trophy hunters discovered a new domain to conquer.

The pack found it increasingly difficult to survive using the old ways. His grandfather had moved the pack closer to civilization and they worked on blending in with humans. The pack thrived and when his father took over, he brought in technology and modern conveniences. He should've been next to carry on, but that was impossible now.

"Uh, yes. My dad loves to. . .watch them." Fuck, that sounded so stupid. He was striking out again and again.

"They are beautiful creatures, especially the arctic wolf with its white coat. Stunning," she said. He couldn't help but smile at that. His mate liked his kind. "You have one as a pet, I believe." Her eyes narrowed, and he smelled her anger.

He wanted to laugh; she wasn't afraid of him, then he remembered what she said before she passed out. He threw his hands up in defense.

"He's not a pet. I'd never chain him up to keep him here." Her brow raised in a *don't bother lying* look. "Really, he comes and goes as he chooses. I just, uh, just watch him."

Dumb-fuck. She had to think he was a complete moron. The isolation had really turned him into a hermit. He'd lost his ability to make logical conversation with females. He really needed to work on his people skills.

He rose from his stool and turned his back to her.

"You need to eat quickly so we can get you back to town before the storm hits." He heard a slight gasp and looked over his shoulder to see her grimace in pain from breathing deeply. He went back and handed her the tea. "Drink all of this. I put a pain reliever in it for you."

She chugged it down and he was thankful she seemed to trust him. She handed him both dishes, their hands touching, and he groaned slightly at the soft touch of her skin against his. Slinging her legs off the bed, she whimpered when she tried to push up with her arms. He set down the plate and cup then grabbed her shoulders, helping her sit up.

"I know it hurts, but I'm going to make sure you get medical help, okay?"

She mouthed a soft thanks then smiled a little. His tiny mate was strong and determined. Good traits for an alpha's mate. No, he told himself. He was not a leader. Not anymore. She pulled her snow coat and pants close to her body, he grabbed the coat by the collar for her to put her arms in. "Where am I?" she asked, standing and moving slowly.

"You're in my cabin. The avalanche dropped you in my l—"

Juliet grabbed his arm. Her hands were damn strong for how small they were. Her eyes were wide with fear and confusion. "Avalanche?" she said. "I don't remember that."

Shit, that worried him a bit. He cupped her face in his hands and studied her eyes. No dilation and they both steadily focused on him. She wasn't in danger of head trauma. Thank god. "I think that's normal for a person in an accident. A lot of times they don't recall what happened. What is the last thing you remember?"

"I was measuring the snow depth, sending an email to the lab. I was supposed to start my vacation after that. But I don't remember leaving."

"You left," he said, "just not how you intended." He couldn't contain the laugh that burst out. Her tumble was not funny but where she landed was.

"How did you find me in all that snow?" she asked.

"You could say you just fell into my lap... literally."

She gave a nod and gazed into his eyes for a moment. Turning carefully, she said, "I'm ready." Her cute nose wiggled.

"Let me grab the keys," he patted his pockets and glanced at the table where he kept change and other knickknacks. Before he moved, his mate sneezed and screamed at the same time, falling onto her hands and knees. He smelled intense pain from her.

He dropped beside her. "Juliet?" She shook her head hanging down, sweat dripping from her face, her arms shook, and he caught her before she face planted on the wood.

EIGHT

J uliet woke under warm blankets. The pillow wasn't hers, but she remembered she was on vacation and not at home. Then she remembered that wasn't the case either. She was in the home of a gorgeous, but strange, man in Alaska.

Only moving her head, she looked around. The fire behind the rock wall was rolling. Heat poured through the gaps. She smelled food but wasn't sure what it was. She was shocked as shit when he offered the plate filled with regular food.

To find out he grew them, completely blew her away. They were in Alaska. They had pretty much a zero-growing season, especially this far north, greenhouse or not. And the fruits. They were delicious.

She'd never thought about drying as a way to preserve food for later. She'd had trail mix with dehydrated fruit and nuts and M&Ms, but never thought of it as real food.

She thought about the man himself. God, he was so hot, her body heated just thinking about him. It had been too long since she had sex. All she could think about was running her tongue across his taut abs. Gliding her hands along the corded muscles of his arms, feeling them wrap around her body and hold her close while he thrust his cock in and out of her.

Shit, she didn't need to get hot and bothered when she could barely breathe. Panting was not a good idea when your ribs hurt. Plus, some things didn't add up. How did he know her ribs hurt when she hadn't told him? It wasn't like there was any physical evidence. And when she mentioned the wolf, he said he'd never chained up the animal. She'd only said something about that to the wolf—yes, the arctic wolf with blue eyes.

She remembered looking into his eyes when they were about to leave for town. They were the same exact blue. His name meant small, mighty wolf. And his thick white hair was the same as the arctic wolf. Holy batshit. Was he a wolf shifter? If what Raven told her about shifters was correct, then the man would be able to smell her pain, smell everything for that matter.

He could hear way beyond a human's ability. That would explain why he could hear her last night though her voice was barely above a whisper. And if he was the wolf who was with her, then he'd know her ribs hurt and... her face about melted off her skull. . .he heard each comment she made about his abs and his ass. She groaned. How embarrassing. Thank god he hadn't mentioned it.

She thought back to how awkward some moments were last night. When he hit his head on the shelf, after he explained his name, when she complimented his cooking. He was so adorable with his flushed cheeks. He seemed so modest and lived simply. She wondered how rustic his life was. Did he have running water? Electricity? She could only see a portion of the home, but she had the feeling there wasn't a kitchen. He filled her dinner plate from containers around the fireplace.

Juliet snuggled deeper into the covers and pictured him in her mind. When he was cutting wood, everything about him was delicious. As he swung the ax, his T-shirt raised, showing off his perfect abs and how low his jeans set on his hips. The top part of that seductive V from his lower stomach down to his sweet spot drew her eyes to his front bulge as well as his rounded ass.

Damn, the bed coverings were becoming too heavy and heated. She smiled at herself for being so silly. She hadn't thought about the opposite sex like this since Raven took her to see the Men Down Under show a year ago. And talk about men. Damn, Aussie men could strip for her anytime.

But now, she could go with an Alaskan man stripping for her. Her girl parts started to tingle. Good to know her sex was still in working order. Only the parts her toy touched, she knew worked. And that only took care of the necessities. This man could do a hell of a lot more than that.

The front door slammed open, scaring her. From her bed, she saw Tevrik standing in the doorway, covered in snow, breathing deeply, chest heaving. His eyes glowed. Was he excited? Holy shit, he could smell her arousal. Her body said, yes, please, but her mind said he was a stranger. Her body told her brain to fuck off.

No, no, she couldn't do anything with him. She didn't know him. But damn, he was hot enough to melt every inch of snow. And after the storm, shit! The snowstorm must have hit while she was passed out. Did that mean she was stuck there with him?

Her fingers ached to touch him, feel his flesh, drag them through his thick hair. Her taste buds wanted in on the action. She could suck him into her mouth, rub her tongue up and down his ridged shaft. Her heart raced, just looking at him.

Tevrik took a deep breath. And that clued in Juliet to what was happening. It was exactly as Raven had said when she met her mates. His glowing eyes, the animalistic manners, deep breathing. Then she was about to come just thinking about him wanting her. She seldom thought of men. None she knew had interested her. She'd have to confirm with Raven but… Tevrik Awulf was her soul mate.

Raven called it just *mate*, but soul mate sounds way more romantic to her. They were destined to meet. That avalanche wasn't an accident. It was meant to bring them together. She would've laughed at that, but right now, her mind and body were focused on the man coming inside the cabin.

He breathed deeply again. He had to know she was turned on. But he walked to the other side of the room. What the fuck? Did he have a stuffy nose?

On the other side of the cabin, something fell, and she heard a low growl. She giggled.

Joy filled her. Was knowing she met the man meant for her reason enough to be happy? She wasn't in love with him, but from what she'd seen so far, it wouldn't be hard. But she wanted it oh, so hard and she meant more than his cock. Raven would be laughing her ass off if she knew what was going on. She had met her mate! Oh, my freakin' god!

She patted her hair to make sure nothing was sticking up. She was sure her makeup was nonexistent. But he wouldn't care about that. Well, at least Raven's mates didn't. They'd take her to bed if she had clown makeup on.

Juliet pushed up in the bed to lean against the headboard. The pain she expected was non-existent. She rubbed her hands along her sides. What the hell happened? She thought she was going to die, it hurt so much.

"Hopefully, you feel better now," Tevrik said, startling her. He stood at the curtain with his worn jeans and T-shirt stretched across his shoulders. He looked too damn yummy. Good thing he belonged to her.

She tilted her head to the side, letting her hair fall over her shoulder. Time to flirt with her man. With a breathy voice she said, "I feel so much better. What did you do to me?"

Tevrik swallowed hard and stepped away. "I'll be back in a second." He hurried out the door, slamming it behind him. Without his coat. If he got cold, he could shift. Arctic wolves were created to withstand the weather this far north.

She kept her eyes on the door, waiting. And waiting. With a huff, she hollered, "Tevrik, get your ass in here pronto."

Within seconds, the door slammed open.

Tevrik stood narrowed-eyed, lips pulled back in a growl. "What's wrong? Are you in danger?"

He was protecting her. "No. I've been waiting for you to come inside with me."

She patted the bed next to her.

"Oh."

She could see the hesitation on his face. Did she smell bad? Was that why he was avoiding her?

Slowly, he shuffled to her bedside and sat. If he were any farther, he'd fall off the mattress. "Now, tell me, how did you cure me?"

"Cure you?" he asked.

"Look at me," she gestured down her upper body, and thankfully, he obeyed, eyes lingering on her breasts, "I can move, talk and breath again. You did something to fix me."

"Oh," he replied, "while you were passed out last night, I worked on you."

She narrowed her eyes at him "Worked on me, how?"

"I figured the main problem wasn't broken ribs as much as the muscles overly contracting, causing pain whenever you moved."

When she passed out the night before, that scared the shit out of him. He didn't want a mate (liar), but he didn't want anything to happen to her.

When he lifted her unconscious body into his arms, he again felt the knots squeezing her sides. He knew what was causing most of the pain.

As she slept, he had spent hours heating water to place hot towels on her sides to warm the muscles, then deeply massaged the knots to get blood flowing, causing the tightness to relax so she could breathe. As the storm raged outside, the tempest inside him roared with his mate in his bed and hurting.

Well before dawn, the muscles over her ribcage released their death grip around her bruised bones. She would be all right in the morning. He hoped most of the pain would be gone by the time she woke.

She smiled. "Wow, handsome and smart." She reached her hand out to touch him and he jerked away. Juliet silently sighed. "Tevrik, it's okay. I won't bite."

He bounced up onto his feet. "Would you like some tea?" he asked.

"Yes," she said. "Tea and breakfast would be great."

He stepped backward. "Yes, breakfast. Food. I can feed you." He passed the hanging curtain then zipped from her sight. Good god, what was she going to do? Obviously, he knew she was his mate. Raven said the shifters knew almost instantly upon meeting someone.

She'd had enough of lying around and swung her legs over the side of the bed. With small steps, she made her way along the fireplace rock wall to the front where Tevrik sat most of the time. From here, she could see the rest of the cabin. Well, what she thought would be the rest of the cabin.

On the other side of the fireplace was a door in the same place the curtain was on her side. Then a second door was in the middle of the wall. This was it? A seven-foot room on each side of the fireplace and two windows.

Tevrik came through the door in the middle of the wall. When he saw her, he nearly choked. "What are you doing up?" He rushed over, setting the cup on an upturned log.

"I just wanted to walk a bit. Look around."

His concern for her dissolved as he lowered his head. "There isn't much to see. I have nothing."

"Are you kidding?" She lifted her arm and turned to point at the incredible hand-carved table by the bed. As soon as she twisted, her sides screamed. She stumbled, ready to hit the floor, but strong arms wrapped around her waist, keeping her steady.

She looked up to see Tevrik inches from her face while he bent to hold her up. She stared into his eyes and got lost.

"Fuck," he growled. "I'm so sorry." He helped her up, then dragged a rocking chair with more detailed carvings toward the fire. "Here, sit."

She lowered to the rocker and slid back. The hard-wood was surprisingly comfortable. The planks conformed to her body instead of her sitting on a non-giving surface. "This is nice. You made this, didn't you?"

Tevrik stared at her, eyes wide. "How did you know?"

She shrugged. "I didn't. I can just picture you sitting on your stool with a piece of tree, whittling away, lost in your thoughts."

He sat on his stool. "Yeah. That's how I pass time during the worst of the weather." Oh, she could totally come up with more enjoyable ways to pass time in winter.

"Have you tried to sell any of your work? It's absolutely amazing."

His smile returned. "You like my stuff?" He meant the furniture, calm down libido.

"Are you kidding?" she replied. "It's stunning. You could bring in a lot of money with just the table alone."

He shrugged. "I don't need much money. I buy very little." He remained quiet as she rocked. Her heart ached for this strong, beautiful man. What kept him here so isolated? What had happened to make him this way? It was a self-imposed isolation, that was for sure.

"Tevrik? Why do you live alone, so far from family and friends? Surely, there is nothing you could have done bad enough to warrant this."

He sighed and looked away. "That's not important. While you were passed out the second time or was it the third," he chuckled, "the snowstorm hit, so you are stuck here for a while longer."

Juliet sat back in her rocker and sighed. At least she would have more time with her mate, and to make him talk to her. She wasn't leaving without him. "How about that breakfast."

NINE

E arlier when he was outside trying to keep his hormones and wolf under control, his wolf caught a whiff of Juliet's arousal and it made him practically rip the door from its hinges to get inside. He had to fight like never before to keep the wolf in. If he shifted in front of her, he'd never see her again after she ran out screaming.

He really needed to get his shit together. He was better than this. He had control over his baser instincts. Or so he thought.

He swore she was trying to seduce him. But why would she? He was a stranger, she was too much temptation.

He heard her voice and he and his wolf were. .

.compelled, for lack of a better word. He hadn't felt that kind of pull since he was with the pack and his father, the alpha, ordered him to do something.

Something must've been wrong. He hauled ass the few feet to the door and threw it open. His wolf came close to the surface, searching for danger. When there was none, it relaxed. She patted the bed beside her, wanting him to sit beside her.

That probably wasn't a good idea. She had such an effect on him. She was beautiful, making his heart thump. And here she sat now, infusing him with the self-respect he didn't deserve. She saw so much in him that wasn't there anymore. Fifteen years ago, perhaps.

What he smelled from her wasn't pity, but pride. She was proud of him even though he had nothing to be proud of. Damn, he loved his mate already. Her heart was good and kind. Wanting to believe the best in him. But she didn't know the truth.

Tevrik rotated out the water kettle and dipped out a cupful and set it next to where he put her mug earlier. He dropped an herb bag into each to seep while he dished out breakfast.

"Mighty wolf," Juliet said. He froze, caught off guard "That's what your names mean, right? You said little, mighty wolf."

His heart warmed. "Yes."

His wolf liked the sound of that too.

Juliet laughed. The sweetest sound he'd ever heard. "I have to say, mighty wolf, I'm amazed with this setup." She gestured at the fireplace.

It was rather ingenious if he said so himself. "When I built this cabin—"

"You, as in you, yourself?" Juliet asked, her jaw hanging from surprise.

"Yes," he smiled, "me, myself." She nodded with an expression showing she was impressed. "Anyway, when I built this, I had no electricity, so I had to come up with a way to eat. Hunger is a great motivator."

She laughed again.

"There was a lot of trial and error, but I finally got something that worked for me."

Juliet sat forward in the rocking chair. "What all do you have attached to the fireplace walls, and why did you use stacked rock like you have?"

"You see how the metal bar with the water pot pivots to move in and out of the fire." She nodded. "It's basically the same on this side, but it's a flat surface to cook food." He swiveled that rod to bring out the griddle. Caribou bacon sizzled. His mouth watered.

"Oh my god," Juliet said, "Is that bacon?"

He nodded. "It's great."

He watched her brows draw together.

"I know there aren't little pink pigs running around up here," she said. "Do I want to know what it's made of?"

He pulled a piece from the griddle's side. "Try it first." She hesitantly took the meat from him and bit off a chunk. Her eyes lit up.

"This is great. There's hardly any fat on it."

"Caribou have very little fat to them," he said.

She winced a bit. "Caribou?" Then she shrugged. "Oh well, it is what it is, and this is good."

Tevrik's heart leapt with lust when she brushed her hand against his. He turned away and pulled berries and dried fruit from containers.

"Okay," his Juliet said, "I can see the berries from the forest, but you have to buy the dried apples and mangos. Alaska doesn't have tropical or fruit trees."

He winked at her. "Nope. I'll show you after we eat." With another full plate, he handed her more than enough sustenance. His wolf was proud, at least.

"How's the weather outside?" she asked after a moment of silent eating.

"The storm has passed for the most part. It dumped a couple feet of snow. Drifts in the back of the cabin are up to the roof."

"Wow," her eyes sparkled at him.

He couldn't help but smile at her. "What?"

"Can we go outside later? I want to walk in it."

"You like the snow? Most women like the beach," he commented.

"One thing you'll learn about me, mighty wolf, is that I am not like any other women." He absolutely agreed with that. "I don't like the beach and hot sun. You can be naked and still sweat your ass off. But in the cold with enough covers, your body will warm up and not sweat through your clothes. Plus, there aren't any animals or trees on a beach. It's just sand that burns the hell out of your feet. And then—"

Tevrik leaned back laughing. "Okay. I get it. You hate the beach."

"I could go on," she said, pushing berries and bacon into her mouth, "but whatever. I love the cold and wilderness."

That surprised the shit out of him. But it was a good surprise. A great surprise.

"How long have you lived here?" she asked.

"Around twelve-thirteen years. Time seems to stop out here," he said.

"Yeah?" Juliet questioned.

He shrugged. "There's no stressful schedule. No Joneses to keep up with." She smiled at his humor.

"What do you do for money?" Juliet asked. "I mean, some of this you bought, right? Like the metal rods."

"Since we're off the grid—"

Juliet sat forward in her chair again. "Completely off?" she said. He watched her to make sure she wasn't in any pain as she moved around.

He gave a serious nod. "Totally. I have no bills like the normal person."

"What? No snowcat ATV insurance?" They both laughed. The thought of a company insuring something meant to go through treacherous terrain seemed silly. "You're completely off the grid. Amazing. How do you. . .get along," she asked.

"I get water from snow and have barrels to collect rainwater. I keep steaks in a box buried in the permafrost which is colder than a normal fridge. The fire heats and cooks. Fat from animals easily becomes oil for the lantern, but I usually work with available daylight."

"But sometimes you have as few as four hours of sun, right?"

"Yes, sometimes it's impractical. But I make do."

"Those would be great days to stay in bed," Juliet joked. His mind went straight into the gutter, imagining himself with his naked mate in a toasty bed. His dick hardened quicker than he could move. Shit. His old jeans didn't allow for much room for that. Shit. Didn't help that he scented her arousal and embarrassment. He glanced at her. Rosy cheeks made her even more adorable.

Tevrik took her empty plate and set it aside. "Let me show you how Alaska has bananas." He held his hand out to help her from the rocking chair. When she took it, his wolf howled with joy. Her skin felt wonderful against his. So smooth, so silky. He wanted to rub her hand all over himself. Okay, that sounded a little weird, but whatever. The best part was that she didn't let go and she showed no sign of pain as she got up.

He opened the door on the south side of the house with the most sun exposure. Juliet gasped when she saw the inside of the greenhouse. "Oh my god. This is amazing, Tevrik." He only shrugged, but his wolf howled with arrogance and pride.

He pointed out the different areas with veggies and melons, showed her the herb table where he prepared teas and, at last, his favorite—the orchard.

"How do you keep the trees so small?" Juliet picked an apple from the branches.

"These are dwarf trees," he answered. "Made to stay small for greenhouses and pots."

She checked out the wood plant containers. "Dang, I don't think I've seen a planter so big."

"It was kind of an experiment at the time and I wasn't sure what size would be best, so I made them big."

She smiled up at him. "You made these too?"

He shrugged off her impressed look. "They're just squares. Nothing hard."

Juliet reached out to the material making up the see-thru walls. "Now I know you didn't make these, unless you've got some factory hiding somewhere." She winked at him.

Heat shot through him, all ending up in his groin. His mate was beautiful. So kind. He saw the sweetness of her heart in her eyes. He didn't deserve such a treasure. She deserved so much better than him. He was a fucking mess. A wolf with no pack. No family. Nothing to offer.

Juliet moved to stand in front of him. "I didn't thank you for saving me."

She kissed his cheek and brushed past him, rubbing her breast against his arm. His dick filled so quickly, he was light-headed and knew how a balloon filled too fast felt like. Fortunately, he wouldn't pop. Or so he thought. He couldn't take the flirting anymore. He grabbed her arm and spun her around.

With her chest against his, he growled. "Enough teasing, I am going to kiss you, if you don't want me to, say it now." He paused only for a couple seconds "Time's up." He bent his head and brushed his lips against hers, she moaned and he couldn't hold back any longer. He rubbed his tongue along the seam of her lips "Open up for me."

Juliet moaned again and Tevrik lifted her and pulled on her legs until she wrapped them around his waist. He could feel the heat of her pussy against his cock, she whimpered and he pulled back. Fuck, now he wasn't getting her out of his head. The taste of her would be embedded forever. But wait.

He wasn't being fair with her. He was leading her on, knowing nothing would come of it. He took a couple steps back and turned back to the greenhouse.

"No," he said in a low, rough growl. "No factories hiding in the snow. One of my friends helped me get the right material and I built it out."

Juliet stood where he left her, he glanced back at her confused expression. She cleared her throat. "Living off Mother Nature, almost completely. Amazing. But. . ."

"But what?" he asked. Thank fuck she wasn't going to mention the kiss. He wanted to pretend it didn't happen. He'd dream about it every night forever.

She leaned against the herb table and crossed her legs. "Do you have to go outside to an outhouse?" Her frown made him smile.

"No, let me show you." He led her to the door beside the fireplace.

She brushed her hand over the stacked stone forming the firewall. "I haven't seen a hearth made of rock like this. It's much prettier." All he saw was her hand rubbing the wall and he imagined what it would feel like on his chest.

"Rock stores the heat during the day and at night when it gets cold, it releases that warmth into the rooms. No need for any other type of heating." He figured out thermal dynamics from living in caves and traveling the mountains.

He opened the restroom door and stepped to the side for her to look in. Of all the things to figure out for living off the grid, the bathroom was the most creative.

"Um," Juliet said, her head tilted, studying the facilities, "how does this all work?"

The toilet was normal except for the much larger tank on the back. Tevrik opened a small window where snow was packed on the outside. He scooped snow into a bucket and dumped that into the tank.

"Oh," Juliet said, "the snow melts down and that water is used to flush. That's smart. Where does it go?"

"Well," he scrubbed his fingers through his hair, "let's just say it's all natural."

"What about. . ." she stuttered through words, "uh, you know. . ." She made a wiping motion with her hand. He smiled to himself. Let's see how she handled this.

"Oh," he replied with a serious face, "a handful of pine needles works well for that, pinecones are better. The hard edges scrape." Her mouth dropped open. "Of course, in the summer, leaves are really good for that. Avoiding poison ivy is ideal. And now, snow is the perfect cleaner. A bit cold, of course."

He almost laughed at Juliet's wide eyes and hand-covered mouth. "But I prefer this." He turned to a wall shelf next to him. His fingers wrapped around the toilet paper roll and lifted it to her. "Biodegradable, of course."

She snatched the roll from him and threw it at him.

"Oh, my god, Tev!" She choked. "You almost gave me a heart attack," she hollered while laughing.

"I thought I'd be wiping my butt with frozen pinecones." He laughed with her, light filling his chest where self-hatred had existed. "Now, get out," she said, "I have to go. Get ready to go outside. I'm ready to play."

The seductive smile on her face just about made him come standing there in front of her.

TEN

J uliet closed the bathroom door after shoving him out. She saw him clench his jaw as she shut the door. Something kept him away from her, and she was determined to find out what and why.

Thank god he had toilet paper though, she had really thought he was serious when he mentioned leaves and shit. When she thought about living off the grid and restrooms, the first thing that came to mind were the latrine type of facilities at the national parks she and her family visited when she was young. They stunk to high heaven and were about as gross as a two-week-old corpse.

That would've been a deal breaker. She and Tevrik would've had a long talk about getting water pipes and using a different, softer material that still came from a tree. Pinecones. She shivered at the thought.

But damn, she was so impressed with how well he was set up with the hearth and greenhouse. Not in her wildest dreams could she have figured out all the genius things he'd done. He was incredibly smart and resourceful.

She thought of Raven's mates, those two dragons would walk around town naked and not think anything of it while women died of heart attacks as they passed. Tevrik was more modest for sure, or at least he was being that way with her. Maybe the isolation on the mountain had something to do with it. But if she lived here, she would be as free as hell. Who needed clothes in a warm cabin anyway? She chuckled at the thought: Welcome home Tevrik. Dinner is served and she didn't mean food.

She needed to find a way to find out why he was avoiding being close to her. Even after the hot kiss, he pulled back. He had to know they were mates. She sensed a playful side of him, but it was buried. This would be a great time to talk to her mother.

Her parents were very demonstrative when it came to their love. PDA was fine with them—and almost all levels of display were fine. That could've been why she was so bold when it came to what she was thinking and wanting.

God, she remembered how embarrassed she was in school when her parents volunteered to chaperone her junior high dance. Oh my god, they sucked face like teenagers behind the bleachers. Juliet was surprised they had their clothes on when they emerged. She never heard the end of it from her friends and teachers. Needless to say, they weren't invited to events that happened at night any longer.

Her mighty wolf was a challenge, and she hadn't had one for a while

She bounded into the room after using the facilities. "Here I am. Let's go outside."

He held her coat up for her to slip her arms into. Her gloves were in her pockets. He moved in front of her and buttoned every button from top to bottom, his fingers brushed against her breasts and she sucked in a gasp. He tied the strings below the zipper that tightened the coat around her legs. Pulled the hood up and grabbed the strings for that.

"Whoa, hold on there a minute, wolf boy," she said, taking the strings from his hands. "If I'm bundled up much more, I won't be able to move." He stepped back, "I'm sorry, I know you said you like the cold but I just wanted to make sure you were going to be warm."

She grabbed his T-shirt and pulled him to her. From there, she planted a big one on him. Wrapping her arms around his neck, she pressed into him, wanting to feel his hard chest against her. She tickled the seam of his lips with her tongue until he opened giving her access to deepen the kiss.

A moan. She wasn't sure if it was her or him. This felt so right. When his arms wrapped around her, pressing her lower back to him, she imagined she could feel his very hard, very long cock against her lower stomach. Her body ignited hotter than the fire in the hearth. He pulled away and walked outside ahead of her. Maybe he just wanted to cool off, or maybe he was avoiding her again.

She followed him out, walking along the front of the home, she scooped up a handful of snow and shaped it into a ball.

Standing around the corner, she waited for him to turn to see where she went. He, of course, could hear her footsteps but she hoped he would come to see what she was up to. Yep, that didn't take long, she thought. Tevrik turned and took one step in her direction.

Taking aim, she threw the ball of white powder,

hitting him dead center of the chest. He was so surprised. "Woman! I can't believe you did that."

She took off running for the back of the house, again, grabbing up a handful of snowflakes. With that move, her ribs shot a streak of pain down her side, reminding her she wasn't completely healed.

She flattened her back against the log wall and watched as his shadow on the glistening ground drew closer to the corner. As he came around, she was in her wind-up and let loose the bomb. It exploded on his chest, again, right in the center. Snow splashed up in his face and he fell backward, back around the corner. She laughed and ran for the woods behind the house. Hopefully, he wouldn't turn the corner quickly and see her.

Hiding behind a thick tree, she watched as Tevrik sneaked along the side of the cabin. He hadn't seen her run to the forest. Instead, he thought she'd moved to the next corner of the cabin. He thought he was being stealthy. He gathered snow into a ball and stood right at the corner, arm raised. With a big growl, he sprang around the side, arm up to deliver his retribution. Not seeing her, he dropped his arm.

"Hey. Where did you go?" He put his nose in the air. No fair, she wanted to shout. Using shifter super-senses was cheating. Tevrik turned, trying to catch the scent. With his back to her, she wadded up another ball. He was a good distance away this time. About the same length as a pitching mound is to home plate in fast-pitch softball, which her team won state her senior year.

She stepped away from the tree, swung her around, and released the torpedo. Juliet held her breath, waiting to see if she got a strike. The white ball splatted against the back of his head. Yes! Woo-hoo. Juliet jumped with joy until Tevrik turned to her.

His eyes glowed. He made a stunning image, reigniting the flame she had when inside a short of time ago. Damn, he was so fucking hot. The growl from Tevrik rumbled deep in his chest. She finally got the wolf to come out and play. Lord knew the serious Tevrik needed to chill for a while.

Up the hill, she ran, ignoring the dull ache in her midsection. It would go away eventually. Pushing off trees, she didn't make it very far when arms wrapped around her waist. She giggled and laughed when he carefully lifted her petite form into the air.

"Damn, woman. You are unpredictable," he said. When her toes touched the pine needles covering the ground, he spun her around and gently backed her against a tree. "Are your ribs okay?" He unzipped her coat and slid his hands inside. "You are so warm."

Juliet wrapped her arms around him and pulled him flush with her. His brows flew up at her boldness, she wanted him now and forever. The wolf shifter made for her. It felt so romantic, a tear almost welled up. She was such a sucker for the mushy stuff.

She tiptoed and kissed him. He grew hard against her lower stomach. Delicious. She wanted a piece of Tevrik pie. To her dismay, Mr. Goody-Two-Shoes stopped rubbing her sides when his thumbs reached the bottom of her breast. He went no higher.

Goddamn, what kept him from taking her? She was giving him all the go ahead signs and he was not taking the bait.

Juliet released her hold around him and laid her hand on top of his on her chest. From there, she scooted his hand over her breast, the nipple hardening from the touch. It had been forever since a man touched her like this. She'd forgotten how great it felt.

Tevrik pause for a second, then his tongue dove into her mouth as both his hands massaged her breasts. Oh, fuck. She could almost come now.

He pressed his hips harder, rocking a tad, his dick rubbing against her mound. She thought about taking this back inside but getting there would ruin the mood. But so would snow up her ass.

Right when she was about to explode, he stepped back. Each panting like they just finished a marathon. His eyes still glowed, hypnotizing. He grabbed her hand.

"Walk with me. I want to show you something," he said. He helped her navigate the rugged ground with fallen trees and damn sticker bushes. Whoever created those fucking things should've been hog-tied and thrown into one.

There was no conversation between them. Didn't need it. Just being in Mother Nature with crisp air was all she needed. Eh, back up a minute. Nature and her wolfman were all she needed.

They topped the ridge where trees were sparse, making the trek much easier. On the other side, the land dipped into a valley with a dry creek bed winding through it. Oh, yes. She could live here and just stare at the beauty. That included the nicely rounded ass walking in front of her.

Tevrik abruptly stopped. Juliet didn't until her nose met his back. She bounced back instinctively. He grunted. "That's what you get for staring at my ass, woman." She nearly fell to the ground laughing. Busted. Caught red-handed. How did he know she was staring? Last she knew shifters didn't have eyes in the back of their heads.

He took a deep breath. "You smell so damn good."

"What?" That caught her off guard. She wasn't used to people telling her she smelled damn good. Especially when she hadn't bathed in days and wore the same clothes since the last shower.

His face flooded red, then paled. "I-I meant your perfume smelled good." Her brow lifted. "Wait. Maybe it's your soap or shampoo."

She tried to make sense of what he was saying. She knew he could scent all of those items, so. . .

"Okay, okay," she said. "Why did we stop?"

"Because something else I'm smelling shouldn't be here."

ELEVEN

Tevrik about shit himself. He let slip a shifter trait telling his mate she smelled good. Whatever she was doing, he loved it. Her arousal was heady, but it was a bit difficult climbing a steep slope with a boner the size of Texas. Hell, he'd walk her around in circles all day just to keep smelling her. Then something else registered.

He stopped, Juliet bumping into him.

The beautiful woman was taking him places he'd never been. Shit, he almost lost it when she moved his hand onto her breast. He wanted to rip her clothes off right there and pound into her against the tree. But he shouldn't have got so wrapped up in her. The snow clearing away, he planned to take her back to town tomorrow.

He had to step back from her to keep control. He hoped the wolf didn't show in his eyes. She would want to know what caused that, then he'd have to tell her about shifters, then he'd be alone as she ran, screaming, thinking he was cuckoo. Or worse yet, a monster.

She probably thought he was nuts, standing there, sniffing. But what he tasted in the back of his throat wasn't good.

"Stay here for a moment. I need to check out something." He picked up a long branch and swept it across the ground as he walked the rocky path they were on. Most of the trail was covered with a thin layer of snow where the rocks were fairly level.

Suddenly, he heard a loud snapping-clang, the limb jolted in his grasp, and rocks and snow flew everywhere.

"Goddammit," he hollered. "If I ever catch this mother fucker, he's dead." He lifted the limb for her to see the metal bear trap dangling on the end. The snare was buried under a thin layer of small rocks, pine needles, and snow. Some of the limb was sheared off. Damn, if his mate would've stepped on that, it would have broken her leg bone, if not dismembering it altogether.

Tevrik removed the trap from the stick and grabbed it with both hands. A snarl on his face, he twisted the shark-like teeth until the device was unusable.

He heard a commotion behind him. When he saw his mate mimicking him with her own branch, his wolf growled to keep their mate safe. Juliet put a fist on her hip.

"Shut it. You said a *moment*, and I gave you a *moment*. Now I'm helping."

In the next half hour, they'd raked the trail and several yards down the slope into the woods, finding three more traps.

"Why would someone plant these things?" she asked. "I mean, they seem sorta antiquated and dangerous as hell."

Tevrik threw his stick down. "I'll show you why. We're almost there." He reached out a hand and she held on. Nothing ever felt so natural as this. How was he going to let her go?

After going off trail, sliding down a couple feet on smooth rock facing, and climbing up another incline, they crested the ridge. He dropped to his knees and dragged Juliet down with him. "Do you see it?"

"All I see is a hole in the canyon wall," she answered.

"Hold on another minute. The sun needs to be higher," he replied. While they waited, he moved her around the side of the mountain, getting closer to the hole about to come into the sun. As she watched, a brown nose attached to a white-ish muzzle poked out from the hole. Then two white, furry balls with legs rolled out.

"Oh my god," Juliet said, "they're all white. It doesn't look like a polar bear, though."

"They're not. These are regular brown bears, but their fur is white, they are very rare." He sighed. "That is why the traps are set. Someone wants what they shouldn't have."

"By god, they better never set another one of those damn things," Juliet said, anger and determination flowing in her voice. "I'll find the bastard and take care of it personally."

Her courage to protect something so important surprised him. But it shouldn't have. Her tenacity was boundless. God help anyone who stood in her way when she had her mindset.

The two cubs were roly-poly with powder-puff bodies. So cute. They tumbled over each other. One falling on its back in the snow, only its four little paws and the bottom of its belly visible. The cubs climbed all over the mother, chewing on her ears, licking her muzzle, but she didn't seem to mind as she lounged in the sun.

"How do you know about them?" Juliet asked.

"I—uh—just stumbled upon them many years ago," he replied. Shit. He couldn't tell her that he found them in his youth when he was homeless and angry with the world. That time in his life he'd rather forget. "The mother has raised several little ones. She comes back to this cave each time."

"She's so big."

"She's bulked up for hibernation. It will start pretty soon."

"The babies are so adorable. I wish I could hold one," she said.

"No, no, no," he replied. "These are for viewing only. Bears are not a good animal to meet in a dark forest."

Her smile turned teasing, she rubbed against him then asked, "What about wolves? Are they dangerous? Especially the arctic wolves?"

His heart nearly crashed through his rib cage. "Why would you ask about them?" His mind raced thinking back to see if he did something to give himself away. Shit, shit, shit.

She shrugged, watching the cubs' antics. "Just thinking about your pet."

"Pet? Oh, right." She took his hand and interlaced their fingers.

Juliet said, "Do you want children?"

All the thoughts in his head were blown away. Including how to talk. Where did that come from? What were they discussing? Weren't they watching bears?

"I haven't thought much about it," he answered.

"I'd like to have my own baseball team," she commented. He felt the blood drain from his face.

"You want nine children?" The last word came out as a squeak.

She laughed. "Maybe not that many. But I want to practice making them every night and every morning."

Aww, shit. His dick was harder than the stones they sat on. He had to adjust himself or have his cock die of strangulation. He wiggled around pretending to move a rock under his ass.

"Tell me about your family," she said.

"Not much to tell," he answered. "I was just like all the other kids in town. Went to school. Got in trouble on a regular basis." He would never lie to her.

"Mom and Dad still live in the same house. I'm guessing, anyway."

"What do you mean by that?" she asked.

He shrugged. "I haven't seen them in a while, so as far as I know, they still live in the same place."

"How long is *a while*?"

Dammit. She would ask these questions now. Maybe he could deflect and change the subject. He looked up at the sky.

"This time of year, sunrise is around 10:30 and sunset is close to 4:30."

"Wow," she said, frowning at him, "only six hours of day. That'll take a bit to get used to. What time is it now?"

"We got out here late," he answered. "I'd say it's around two." He scooted down the incline they sat on to watch the bears. "There is something else I'd like to show you." He held his hand out. Hers fit perfectly inside his.

"Another surprise?" Getting to her feet, she leaned into him and he kissed her again. Fuck, he loved kissing her. An amazing rush of adrenaline and emotions coursed through him. And a shit load of hormones—horny hormones.

His dick was on a rollercoaster ride from hell. Soft, hard, semi-hard, hard as hell, standing at attention. Right now, he wanted that coaster to plunge into a dark, warm tunnel with tight walls that would squeeze him till he came.

His hands slid down her back to cup her ass. Her legs wrapped around his waist, perfectly placed for her to slide down onto his cock. Up and down. In and out. Hot, tight. He fought the urge to press her to a tree and yank down her pants. Fuck, she was wet and wanting him. His wolf wanted to claim their mate and get on with those children he never thought much about.

That idea pleased him. Keeping her pregnant for several years, starting their family fast—wait. No. She deserved someone so much better than he was. Someone who could provide a decent home, not a two-room shack; someone who had modern conveniences, not using the permafrost as a fridge or dumping snow into the toilet tank to flush.

No. He couldn't trap her in what had become of his life. All because of one mistake.

He pulled away from the kiss, as much as he hated to.

TWELVE

Hand in hand walking through the forest, Juliet asked questions about his life while he sidestepped as many of them as he could. Something happened that he wasn't telling her. Something in his past haunted him to this day. In order for him to heal from the pain, he needed to get the poison, the toxin, of the memories out.

Now he wanted to know everything about her. She really was boring. She told him about her job at the snow company which included measuring snow height as well as stats on glaciers. "Well, I almost died twice."

He jerked around so quickly, she nearly lost her footing on the rocky slope.

"Died? Twice?" he breathed, grabbing her shoulders. He may have said only two words, but his eyes told her so much more. She saw fear, panic, concern, but mostly she saw love. Was it possible to fall head over heels in twenty-four hours? Well, she just did.

Juliet wrapped her arms around his neck and kissed him for all she was worth. She wanted him to know she loved him, too, by her actions. He pressed her against him and he felt so good. His body heat radiated out the collar of his coat. The smell of pine, musk, fresh air. He was good enough to eat. If she got her way, tonight she would be full of him in more ways than one.

He pulled away from the kiss much too soon for her taste. Why was he always stepping back from her? Any other man would've nailed her to a tree twice already. Was she mistaken about seeing love in his eyes? No, he was her mate. He was born to love her. If Raven made up all this shifter crap and fed her a line of bullshit, she would so kill her best friend, dragon mates or not.

He continued to guide her through the forest for at least an hour. He said he wanted to show her something, but she wondered if he'd forgotten about that.

"Tell me how you almost died once," he asked.

"Well. . ." Juliet went into the story about her

discovering mercury poisoning in the folks of Antler. She had to admit it was rather stupid to confront the man causing the problem head on with accusations. But that was the kind of person she was. No beating around the bush, small talk crap. It was *get down to business and fix the hitch right now.*

Right after that, she found herself locked up in the back room of the sheriff's office for a week until Raven rescued her.

After relaying that scary time in her life, Tevrik remained quiet. Something bothered him, but he wasn't sharing. The reason why smacked her upside the head. He'd been living alone for over a decade. He wasn't used to talking to others to work out problems. Duh. They'd have to work on that. Communication was the most important aspect of a relationship. Well, after sex.

The woods were starting to get darker. The sun had traveled its short distance, ready to take its rest for the night. They emerged from the trees onto a flat area of stone. Looking around, Juliet was amazed at the beauty.

The valley below them was hundreds of feet down, filled with coniferous trees and a creek that was mostly dry. She could see for miles from their towering location.

She said, "I've never seen anything so awe-inspiring. It takes my breath away."

"Don't lose too much air. You haven't seen what we came for yet." He turned her in the opposite direction. He was right. More beauty than she could take in spread in front of them.

The mountain range ran westward. Several peaks were higher than where they stood. In the dip between two massive pointy mounds, half of a white-hot orb showered fire across the sky. Along the sides of the slopes, liquid gold flowed like molten lava.

Juliet leaned into her mate. He snuggled round her, making her feel safe and loved. They stood quietly watching the changing hues. When the sun disappeared behind the mountains, the sky burned like hell had open its gates to the clouds.

Wisps of yellow and orange streaked the shadowy scape. Tevrik tugged on her. "We need to go. It will get pitch black fast. We're not far from the cabin. But it's a long way down."

She followed behind, connected to him with fingers linked. They hurried back the way they came through the woods. He was right about the dark coming on fast. She knew his shifter eyes were much better at night than humans'. She put her trust in him.

"Hold up a minute." He lifted his nose slightly. "Turn around." He walked past her, leading her away.

"Wait. Why are we going a different way?" When he didn't answer, she yanked on his arm. "Tevrik, what's back there that you don't want me to see?"

With a sigh, he said, "It's more like I don't want them seeing you."

"Huh?" was her only response to his strange wording.

"Wolves, Juliet."

"What about them?" Wolves were fine. Hell, he was a wolf. What was the big deal?

He spun around and faced her. "Are you serious? Wolves could attack you."

She cozied up to him. "That's what I'm hoping for later."

He stepped back. "What?"

Now she said, "Are *you* serious? You don't get what I just said?"

He turned around and continued through the trees, heading more in a downward direction. "We're taking a different route home. It's faster anyway."

"Oh, why didn't we go that way to begin with?" she asked. Not that she didn't want to spend time with him. Just curious.

He helped her over a log bound on both sides with wild brush.

"Because it can be dangerous," he answered.

"How so?"

The trees suddenly disappeared like someone drew a line and everything on that side simply vanished, except the tilted muddy ground.

"What happened here?" she asked.

"This is the edge of a rockslide. Took out all the trees and topsoil, leaving only slippery mud from the snow earlier." He pointed to a path she could barely see in the oncoming night. "That's the trail we want to get to."

Stepping forward, she said, "Well, let's—" When her step came down on the mud, the angle of the slope was too much for her boots to cling to. Her leg slid out from under her as she skidded unhindered along the incline. She grabbed at rock edges, but her fingers weren't strong enough to overcome her downward fall. Her slick vinyl coat only made the issue worse.

Even though it was night, the twilight was bright enough for her to see what lay at the end of her slide —a cliff where the rock cut off, straight down for hundreds of feet.

Panic clawed at her brain, but she held a barrier

around her logical mind. How could she slow her body's momentum? She twisted sideways, rotating her hips so the length of her boots dragged across the ground, slowing her some, but not enough to keep from going over the edge.

Nothing else came to mind to save her. This was her end. A jolt of adrenaline, maybe overwhelming fear, blasted from the center of her chest, but other than that, she felt calm. At least she would die in the place she liked being the most. Much better to die by falling off a cliff than a shark ripping your leg off and slowly bleeding to death.

In the corner of her eye, she saw a white streak dash out of the woods toward her. Next thing she knew, her body was moving sideways instead of down. She tried to see who was dragging her by her coat's hood but couldn't see anything.

Next, she was flung in a circular arc then hit rock that wasn't slick. She rolled a few times and came to a stop, staring at the darkening sky. After a moment, a familiar floppy tongue lapped at her face.

She sat up, forcing the white wolf away from her face. "I'm okay. I'm okay." The wolf stared at her a minute then ran up the path, disappearing into the darkness. She lay back, her ribs hurting once again.

Then she realized why she couldn't see the wolf's tail when he was dragging her.

Hurried footsteps reached her ears before her eyes made out Tevrik, barefoot, his jeans busted open in front, but still on. In an instant, he was on the ground next to her, scooping her up, and rolled her on top of him. He pressed her head to his chest, his other arm around her waist, squeezing.

Her body moved up and down with each of his deep breaths. His body began to shake. Oh, wait. That was her. She brought forward her scientific mind, fighting the shock setting in wanting to take her *cool as a cucumber* status.

An image of the cucumbers in Tevrik's greenhouse came to mind. She thought about how warm the area was, the smell of the soil, all the short green plants, and Tevrik beside her. At the herb table, his upper arm brushed hers. It was one of their first touches. Well, for her. During the previous night, he massaged the muscles on her ribs to relax so she could breathe. Right now, she felt those same muscles tightening along her ribs.

"Tevrik," she whispered, "we need to get home." He rolled up and was on his feet with her cradled in his arms. Without a word, he walked down the path, doing his best not to slide too much. This rock was crumbled gravel instead of the smooth, slippery face of the rockslide patch.

She would normally ask to walk herself, but now she was afraid her legs wouldn't hold her up. After several minutes of descending the mountainside, huge boulders and rock lay in a heap. Glancing up the slope, she saw the flat section of rock next to the forest. This was where she would have landed had Tevrik not saved her.

She wrapped an arm over his shoulder and cried onto his bare chest.

THIRTEEN

Tevrik carried his mate in his arms down the path toward home. He had never been so scared in his life. His body was moving before his mind registered what was happening. Juliet was there and gone in a blink.

His alpha wolf had been in control with no complaint from him. He shifted midair, which he didn't know he could do. His shirt was shredded, but his jeans stretched enough to contain the back end of him.

With the cliff coming fast, his wolf darted from the forest, his claws clinging to the cracks and crevices too small for fingertips to catch. Then, he almost missed her, biting down on the hood as she slid past. The only reason he was able to get close, was her fast thinking.

As her boots scraped over the rock, her course changed from straight down to an angle toward the path. He thanked whatever deity was watching over them for the much-needed help.

Even with his alpha strength, claws, and forward momentum, eventually, gravity took its hold. He was close enough to the trail that if he flung her toward safety, her body should reach the gravel before resuming its plunge. He watched through wolfen eyes as his mate hit the rocks and rolled. With his load gone, he found he could run faster, overcoming some of the downward pull.

So many emotions slammed him as he carried his only love, his reason for living, toward home. His lonely life had not even come close to preparing him for such a barrage. For the longest time, he had been lost in his own pity party to feel much. He woke in the morning, kept busy until sundown, then went to bed. He would go for months without saying a hundred words.

She had gifted so much to him. Reminding him what it felt like to care for someone, to love and cherish. He needed to decide whether he would be selfish and keep her to himself or let her go to find someone who could give her what she deserved.

He'd worry about that later. Right now, his mate needed him, and *he* needed his mate.

After entering the small home, he placed her on her feet in front of the fire. He wiped mud off the zipper pull and the metal teeth as he opened her now brown coat. He dropped it on the floor. From a chest at the end of the bed, he withdrew two worn blankets. One he draped over a stool and put next to the fire and the other he wrapped around her.

Crouching, he unburied the laces of her boots and pulled them off with her socks. When he stood, he locked eyes with her. Her face was smeared with muck, but she was still beautiful. His hands snaked through the front of the blanket opening and found her belt. He unbuckled and unbuttoned the pants then slid the mud-caked material down and off her legs.

She turned her back to him and offered the blanket corners for him to hold. Her delicate arms pulled from her top, then she unhooked her bra, adding it to the pile on the floor. Tevrik wrapped the blanket around her and scooped her up into his arms.

Juliet winced a little. Her ribs probably bothered her again. He'd take care of that in a minute. He placed her in the rocking chair she sat in earlier then stoked the fire to make sure the room would be warm enough. It would all be perfect. It had to be.

This night, he would remember for the rest of his life. This night, he would make love to the only woman he would ever hold. This night would be the last he ever had with her. It must last him a lifetime.

At the back of the greenhouse, he flipped over a tub he'd carved out a long time ago and filled it with snow piled up along the back of the house. He then carried it through to the front and set it before the fire.

Swinging the water kettle out of the embers, he grabbed a padded leather mitt and poured steaming water onto the snow. When he was finished, he put his hand in to test the temperature. He would never chance scalding her silky skin.

When she started to get up from the chair, he raised a hand for her to stop. Seeing confusion on her face, he grinned and lifted her from the rocker. From there, he placed her in the tub, blanket and all.

From a shelf on the front wall of the fire, he took down a handful of boiled soapberries and a sea sponge that had washed ashore from the Beaufort Sea. That journey was long ago when he had yet to find himself. But he remembered it like it was last week.

In clothes that he'd found in a half-buried back-pack in the forest a while back, he walked the rocky shoreline of the northern flats of the Book range. He'd been on the run for a long time, not caring what happened to himself. If not for his wolf forcing him to feed and sleep, he wouldn't have gotten as far as he had.

When he had come across the sponge camped out on the rocks, he studied it for a while.

He realized then that there was so much he didn't know about the world he lived in. The diverse people, countries, species, foods. So much of all of it unknown. There, he came to a crossroad in his young life.

He'd run from all he knew that one unforgettable day. So young, so stupid. Ran from family, friends, security, love, but most of all from what he had failed to do. His past few years of nomadic lifestyle had taught him much through trial and error, especially how to live through the brutal sub-arctic weather. He was so young that fateful day, but survival matured him faster than anything else could have.

He was truly alone for the first time in his life.

Standing at the brink of the northern Alaska sea, sponge in hand, he had a choice of wandering the land for the rest of his days, which wouldn't be many in that climate, or he could own up to his faults and failures like a man and try to salvage a life from shattered remains. He always thought he'd eventually go home, but the longer he held out, the more awkward and embarrassing the whole thing became. His pride wouldn't let him show so much weakness.

He had made a life-changing decision that day and kept the sponge as a reminder. Now the sponge would mark the night he chose the road less taken.

Soapberries in hand, he knelt beside the carved-out mini-tub and rubbed his hands together to create a frothy lather that he spread over her back and sides. He brushed the soaked sponge across her skin that rewarded him with a sultry moan from his mate.

His dick had been hard for the last ten minutes, so becoming harder now was no big deal. The comfort and emotional calmness for his mate was.

He rubbed his palms over her ribs, feeling for the knots that caused her pain. Having her submersed in hot water was better than draping hot towels over her clothes like he had done the night before to loosen the muscles. With the heel of his hand, he pressed on each knot until it released its death grip around the injured area.

When her ribcage was smooth, she took a deep breath and slid down in the water, her knees coming up higher. Grabbing a large pot, he filled it with bath-water then set it on a footstool behind her head. He crushed more berries and worked the soap through her mud-crusted hair. Her beautiful golden strands returned to their previous luster after a second pot of water.

Wringing out her hair, he feathered a kiss on her shoulder. He took her shudder as permission to continue. Following each lathering and rinsing, he placed a kiss on that section of her skin. First her shoulders, then up her sweet neck, he brushed his lips, barely tasting the flesh. Holding her arm above the water, he rubbed the sponge in small circles, massaging as he cleaned.

His kisses trailed up her limb, his eyes locked on hers the entire time. What he read from them humbled him. The love and desire were almost too much to take. If the tub were bigger, he might have jumped in with her. But his wooden creation was definitely for one body.

Plus, this was all about her. His way to worship the goddess she was. His way of ensuring to himself that she was alive and with him. She could've so easily not have been.

He lifted one of her legs and scrubbed above the ankle where mud had gotten past her boots. Another kiss had goose bumps popping up her skin. So sweet, so perfect. Before letting her go, he massaged her sides one last time to make sure he muscles were relaxed and causing no pain.

After he had touched, kissed, every part of her that the bath allowed, he retrieved the blanket he had draped over the stool earlier. By now, it was warm and toasty to keep his mate comfortable while he tucked her into bed.

He held the covering up as she stood, giving her the privacy she needed. He wasn't sure how shy his mate was. She was bold with what she wanted, but when it came right down to it, would she still be the female alpha she'd shown to be? He'd find out, hopefully. It would all be based on what she wanted. When she stepped out of the tub, she took his hand and led him to the bed.

Soft light seeped through the notches in the rock wall, making the space much too hot for him if he was going to stand next to her in only a towel. She stared into his eyes. Was she wanting to ask him a question? They hadn't said a word since the near fatality. Nothing he could say would express what he felt, which was every emotion possible. To his surprise, she opened the blanket around her and let it fall to the floor.

FOURTEEN

Juliet had never felt so loved as she had at the hands of her mate. She was right pegging him as born for her. She had never fallen in love before and now she was buried in it without so much as a first date. None of that courting stuff was necessary. Her heart told her he was the one. And his actions showed her what he wasn't saying. Who needed words when you could read it in the eyes?

Yes, this would be their first night together of many more to come. She wanted his touches to reaffirm she was here. Nothing brings a person more alive than almost dying. And she wanted to feel life and all the sensations this man would bring her.

Standing beside the bed with Tevrik in front of

her, she dropped the blanket, letting him know, without doubt, what she wanted. She almost laughed when his eyes widened and tried not to scan down her body, but they did.

She knelt and pulled off his muddy jeans. As suspected, he was commando. What rugged mountain man wore underwear? Not that she really knew, but hers wouldn't. He'd see them as unnecessary and just something else to wash.

He'd cleaned the crud off his chest from her ruined coat, so he was good enough to eat. Time to partake in the meal. Juliet grabbed him around the shirt and pulled his lips to hers. His mouth was hot, she wanted more of him. Needed more of him.

Juliet loved the feel of his lips on hers. If she'd had any doubt about wanting him, it had gone out the window at that point. The feral way his gaze swept her face made her shiver in need.

"I'm going to take what's mine, Juliet. You." His words skyrocketed her need off this planet.

Desire and lust pushed her at this point. Then his lips were all over her, not the soft, sweet kisses from her bath but ones that left her trembling with need. He gently laid her on the bed and crawled over her and started kissing his way down her body again.

He bit down on her belly. His downward travels

stopped when he reached her bare pussy. He licked her inner thigh and she groaned. "I've been dreaming of having a taste of you, Juliet. So badly."

She bit her lip. Words stuck in her throat. Her legs spread wider as if to give him the hint. His lip curled in a fuck-a-licious grin.

"Know what I want?" He licked closer to her pussy but not close enough. God, that was nowhere near close enough and she might lose her mind if he didn't hurry it up. She almost yelled at him. Did he fucking need a map? He was bent on torturing her.

Jesus, how she needed to come. Her legs already shook from her lack of control over her muscles.

He was going to kill her from sexual frustration. She lifted her hands to her nipples and pinched, the bite of pain adding to the ever-growing need in her body.

"I want to feel your pussy soaking my face."

Oh. My. God.

A sharp electric current shot right to her clit, making it twitch. Her body trembled and all he'd done was a few licks around her pussy. At this rate, she'd never make it another five minutes.

He licked at the crease between her pussy and her leg. So close but still so far.

"Please, Tevrik," she moaned. She let go of her nipples and gripped clumps of his short hair.

"Ah, fuck, baby." He licked over her pussy lips. "Wiggle those hips and show me how much you like my tongue on your clit."

She whimpered, pressing close to his mouth—if that were possible—and waited. If he didn't do more, she'd be the first woman she knew to come with words alone.

"You are so fucking gorgeous, Juliet. I'm so hard seeing you slick, hot, and wet," he groaned. He rubbed his face on her slick folds. "You smell delicious, like an amazing memory. Only you're real and this won't be a dream that goes away when I wake up. You'll be mine. All mine."

The ragged sounds of her breaths filled her ears. She couldn't think. All she could do was hope he'd lick her again. Soon.

She spread her legs even wider. "Tevrik . . ."

His gaze caught hers at the moment he flattened his tongue and licked a slow trail up to her clit. It ended with an agonizing suck of her tiny hard nub.

"Yesss."

Her nipples puckered so damn tight.

Everything was perfect as long as he was doing those wonderful things to her body.

Tevrik licked her clit in quick hard swipes. One after another, they left her breathless and begging.

Her body tensed so fast it caught her off guard.

"Oh . . . oh . . . my . . ." She choked the words out.

Tevrik reached his hands up to cup her breasts and tweak her nipples. The feel of his calloused fingers added a new dimension of painful pleasure. Desire flowed through her in waves of heat and fire, and a storm raged in her core, pushing her closer to the edge. She rocked her hips, rolling them back and forth on his face.

"That's it," he muttered between licks and sucks. "Ride my face."

She liked the sound of his voice. Liked the way he encouraged her to be naughty. Not that any encouragement was necessary. She was one lick away from coming on his face and that thought alone made her even hotter.

"Come, baby." He pushed his tongue into her sex. She almost came on the spot. "Once you do, I promise to lick up every bit of your sweetness."

She wanted that oh so badly. Her body vibrated with the need to ride the orgasm wave. She was at the peak; a little push and she'd go over.

Tevrik's actions got more aggressive. He pressed his tongue over her clit and then sucked her harder.

Her body trembled with his low growl over her sensitive flesh. That definitely caught her off guard and pushed her into the abyss.

She screamed. Her back bowed. Her head thrashed with the eruption of pleasure rushing her body.

Her breath reeled, pumping hard into her lungs. She kept coming, her orgasms pushing each other until she was spent and almost falling asleep from the amount of energy she'd expended.

He pulled her into his arms and held her close.

"Tell me what you want now, beautiful."

She rolled him onto his back and placed a leg on either side of him and slid his cock into her entrance.

"You. I want you. Deep."

She rode him hard, her body gliding up and down and tensing with every slide down. He was hot and thick, pulsing deep inside her. He gripped her hips with every single slam down.

"Do it, baby. Ride me."

She wiggled more. He helped her, biting his fingers into her hips and lifting and dropping her on his cock.

With every slam, she moaned and whimpered his name. He grunted, telling her how much he loved her curves. How gorgeous her body was. Then she was going faster and faster, her body slick with perspiration and the tension inside her ready to snap.

She slammed down a final time, taking him as deep as she could. Pleasure flowed as tightness snapped.

He growled, lifting his hips, driving deeper into her. His cock felt harder, hotter, and bigger inside her. Then he was spilling his seed into her. She took large gulps of air while her pussy contracted around his cock.

"That's it, baby. Take it. Take me." He yanked her head down and met her lips for a ferocious kiss.

FIFTEEN

Tevrik woke with a warm body tucked into him. The smell of soapberries filled his senses. His eyes opened to see a head of blond hair, tangled and a mess, on his pillow. It was true; he wasn't dreaming. His mate was here. His heart expanded with so much happiness. Then he remembered he had to send her away. His chest tightened, constricting his breathing.

It was the right thing to do. Hell, he couldn't even keep her safe for a full twenty-four hours. She almost died on him last night. He would've followed her to the grave had that been the case. His wolf thought it strange that he was willing to die with her, but not willing to live with her.

Dammit, he didn't want her to go. He wanted to

keep her beside him forever. But he had nothing to offer her. Not even a real home to live in. If only that fucking hunter hadn't been around, his life would be completely different.

He would've had prestige, power, and wealth as the pack leader. His father had always said he would retire early so Mom and he could travel. And to think that Tevrik thought he was ready to take his father's place. Stupid, idiotic, fucking teenager. He knew nothing then. Nothing.

Now he was spending the rest of his life paying for it. No. He wouldn't condemn his mate to his fate. He'd let her go to find a real life. His wolf howled in his head, but it knew Tevrik was right. This wasn't the time to be selfish, after all this time he matured, but he hadn't atoned for his mistakes. The mistakes of youth for which the adult must pay.

Juliet moved in his arms, the little minx wiggling her wonderful ass against his crotch. Even after making love three times that night, he was hard in an instant, ready to take her. She moaned and pushed back into him when he pressed his filled cock to her ass.

"Good morning, beautiful. How are you feeling?" he asked.

"Mmm," she hummed, "deliciously sore."

He realized he was squeezing her upper body and whipped his arms from her to stop the pain in her ribs. She laughed and grabbed his hand hovering over her. "No, silly. Not here. Down there." She twitched her hips. "I love it."

A huge sense of satisfaction rolled through him knowing he had made his mate happy. He snuggled more into her, relishing her warmth and scent.

"Tell me about your family again," Juliet said. His knee-jerk reaction had him pulling away from her.

"Why?" he answered.

She rolled over to face him. "Because there's something going on there you don't want to talk about."

He schooled his face to keep his anger and shame hidden. "You're right. I don't want to talk about it."

"But you have to if you want things to get better," she came back.

"What do you mean, get better? I'm happy with things as they are."

"Tevrik Awulf," she reprimanded, "you can't bullshit a bullshitter. I see right through that poker face of yours. You're angry and hurt because of something. You can't begin healing until you open up to let the pain go."

Dammit, he was a fucking open book to her. He

should've known he couldn't hide anything from his mate. Not only was she caring, but smart. Too smart for him to try to fool. He sighed and buried his face in her hair.

"It's not anything really," he said. "When I was seventeen, we had. . .a falling out, of sorts." When he kissed her neck, hoping to entice her mind on something else, she pulled his earlobe.

"I know what you're trying, buddy, and it ain't working. When was the last time you saw your family?"

He sighed again. "When I was seventeen."

Juliet bolted up, covers slipping down her chest until her hand caught them. "That has to be fifteen years ago at least."

"Yeah," he nodded, "that's about right."

She fell back onto the pillow. "Tevrik, that's horrible. You must miss them so much." Her warm hand rubbed his cheek. He kissed her palm and shrugged.

"Like the entire town, I'm sure they have no desire to see me again. So I've stayed away." His thoughts went to what Petey and James said the other day: The pack is better off without you. No one wants you around.

"The town?" she asked. "How can a whole town not want you back? What did you do? Rob a bank?"

He laughed. "If only it had been that simple. Money is easy to return."

"What happened that you couldn't return?" she replied.

"Juliet," he groaned, "let it go. Let's make love one last time before I take you to the airport."

"Take me to the airport?" She pulled away from him and sat up. "You want me to go?"

"Juliet—"

"Was that the plan all along?" she snapped. "Get into my pants then send me on my merry fucking way?"

"Yes," he shook his head, confused on what happened to draw her anger, "wait. I meant no."

She whipped the blankets off and shot out of the bed. "I get it. Being out here alone, any woman who comes along, you take advantage of."

"No, Juliet. That's not true," he said, climbing out of bed after her. She turned the corner of the fireplace and stopped.

"You washed my clothes for me?" The hurt in her voice tore at him. He had gotten up while she slept during the night and scrubbed down her muddy garments and draped them in front of the fire to dry. She hurried away from him. "Never mind. Thank you." The anger was back.

Fuck. He had to smooth this over. "Juliet, listen—"

"No," she replied, "I don't want to hear another word from your mouth."

"Juliet, please," he said.

"This is over and I don't want to see you again." She grabbed her clothes and changed in the bathroom. "And the sad thing is I thought we were soul mates. God, am I a fucking idiot or what?"

Soul mates? Did she mean mates? How could she know that? No, soul mates were just a romantic idea humans had. She didn't mean shifter mates. Well, he didn't have to worry about her running from finding out what he was.

After dressing, she stomped across the cabin and out the front door.

Fuck. Where the hell was she going? Tevrik put on clothes and started up his snowcat. Having gone into town not too long ago, it started up right away. He saw her on the tundra, not too far. He put the vehicle in gear and headed her way.

Was he doing the right thing? With her big fancy job, he was sure she would hate giving all that up to be with him. Yes, he was doing the right thing. She would see in hindsight that he was doing this for her.

God knows it wasn't for him. He and his wolf were slowly dying inside.

He pulled up alongside her and leaned over to open the passenger door.

"Juliet, let's talk about this," he said.

"What is there to talk about?" she hollered, still walking. "The roads are clear and it's time for me to get back to my life."

Yes, that was what needed to happen, but he couldn't say it out loud. That would make it real. "Juliet, please, get in."

"No," she said, not even looking at him.

"You're going the wrong way."

After a few more steps, she stopped and huffed. "Fine. But I don't want to hear one word from you or I'm out."

He slid his fingers across his lips like he was zipping them closed. She climbed inside and closed the door. He turned the snowcat around and headed the other direction. He asked, "Do you need to get the truck you drove up to your snow location?"

She chewed on her lower lip, gazing out the window. "I'll call the rental place and have them get it. I want to be gone as soon as possible." Her words were short and sharp, cutting into him.

But really, how did he think she was going to

react? She never said anything about them staying together. Never said anything about moving up here.

What the fuck was he doing? Of all times he needed his mother and father, this would be it. He needed advice on something he had no idea how to fix. Maybe it was now beyond being repaired.

SIXTEEN

The man infuriated her. Treated her like a whore, kicking her out of bed the next morning. Well, she wasn't having that. She'd leave first. She didn't need him, but she wanted him. Two different things.

She sat in the warm snow vehicle as the wolf boy drove toward town. It was about a two-hour journey and she was exhausted from frustration and a broken heart. Not to mention hungry. As things started to become familiar, she knew they were close to town.

"Can we stop at the general store," she asked, "so I can get a couple protein bars and juice? Then you can drop me off at the condo my company rents. My stuff is there. You don't have to go all the way to the airport."

Tears rolled down her cheeks, but she kept her face turned toward the window. No reason to let him know how badly she was hurting inside. Wait. He was a damn shifter. He could smell exactly how she felt, yet he offered no words of consolation or comfort. But she did tell him not to say a word. She let a heavy sigh. This was so complicated.

Tevrik parked in the small lot for the store. Instead of waiting for him, she opened her own door and hopped out. Being a good distance from the mountains, the air was warmer and the breeze wasn't so constant.

He held the store door open for her and she walked through with a mumbled *thank you*. The inside was bigger than what it looked on the outside. The place was an eclectic mix of merchandise from food to clothes and toys to caribou mating calls.

Mating calls. Whatever. She didn't believe in mates anymore. What Raven told her about being inseparable wasn't correct. Maybe with her men, but not with Tevrik. She missed Raven and wanted to talk to her.

She hadn't thought about her cell phone until now. Not that there was a cell signal where they were in the mountains. The device she used to transmit the data to the lab worked off stationary satellites—made especially for remote locations with no coverage. That she knew was lost in the avalanche. But what about her personal phone.

Oh, shit. She'd better call Raven soon. The last time Juliet hadn't responded to her messages, Raven came all the way to Alaska looking for her. Then, when Raven ignored her mother's messages, her mom brought the entire Alaskan national guard to rescue them. She didn't want a repeat of that.

Juliet patted her coat's big outside pockets and outer zipper cubbyholes. Finding nothing, she felt around inside. In the closed breast pocket, something small and hard—several somethings, for that matter—rolled around.

She unzipped the pocket and pulled out a handful of the contents. When she saw the nuggets sparkling in her hand, memories flooded her mind. Memories that had been lost with the avalanche she didn't remember, but now recalled.

"Oh my god." She remembered the dollar amount could be a million dollars. "Tevrik!" she shouted, drawing the attention of other customers. She didn't give a shit. She was rich. "Tevrik!" At the end of an aisle at the back of the store, he tore around the end of the row, searching for her. His eyes glowed. She had scared him. She'd apologize, but first things first.

She was so excited, she couldn't think of what to say. She just held her hand out, bouncing on her toes. Tevrik picked up a piece and studied it.

"This is the biggest nugget of gold I've ever seen," he said. "All of these are huge. Where did you get these?"

"I remember it all, Tevrik," she spewed. "Before the avalanche, I found a small cave and inside were many bags filled with gold. It's old. I can't believe I forgot something this momentous."

"Do you remember where the cave is?" he asked.

She nodded. "It's just below where the snow measuring stick is." She jumped up and down, too excited to stand still.

"Okay," he said, taking the protein bars and bottle of juice from her other hand, "let me pay for this and we can talk about this in a private location." He glanced around as if looking for spies.

"Right," Juliet said, "good idea. I'll meet you outside at the snowcat." She dropped the gold back into the pocket. "Isn't this so exciting? It's like finding lost treasure."

He laughed at her overabundant exuberance. "I'll be up front." He walked away and she took a deep breath. With her anger forgotten, she was giddy with excitement. But she needed to get herself under control.

"Excuse me, miss," a voice behind her said. She turned to see a store employee standing a few feet away. The nametag on his shirt read Petey. "I was in the next aisle and couldn't help but overhear you found bags of gold."

A smile so big spread on her face that her cheeks hurt. "Sorry. I was rather loud."

He shrugged. "Congrats on that. You should compare your findings to some of the legends we have around here. You could've found some old miner's lost fortune."

"I'll do that. Thank you for the advice," she replied.

He blushed a little. "I came over to ask if you would help me carry in a bulky box. I hurt my hip and I'm afraid I'll bump something."

"Sure." She glanced back toward Tevrik. He was in line to checkout. This would take just a moment and they'd find a quiet place to talk.

Maybe she should flat out tell him how she felt. Men were sometimes the densest creatures on the planet. Perhaps he didn't catch all the hints she had sent him over the past day. She could invite him to her place for a while until she got a new work schedule that would allow her to work and travel from the cabin. Hell, he could just move in with her if he was willing to give up what he had here. If it were her, she'd find it hard to give up.

Juliet followed Petey toward a door that read Employees Only.

"It's here on the other side of the door," he said, "I couldn't get it through on my own." He held to door open for her. As she passed him, heading into the warehouse, a sharp pain radiated from the back of her skull and everything went black.

SEVENTEEN

Tevrik stood in line at the small store check-out and shook his head. How in the hell did his mate find gold is such big chunks? He'd only seen nuggets that large in pictures from the 1800s.

But what astounded him the most was the huge smile on her face and how lit up with joy she was. How could he go on never seeing that again? He was a total jackass for how he'd handled this. If only he wasn't in exile. Well, that wasn't completely correct.

He ran away as a dumb kid, unable to face the disappointment and accusations that his pack would undoubtedly throw on him for failing. He'd cast himself into isolation, refusing the luxuries of modern man. All that making him an unsuitable companion for his mate. Then it dawned on him.

Just because he had chosen to live in seclusion for over a decade didn't mean he had to stay there until he died. What if he followed Juliet instead of her having to stay with him? Women were independent creatures nowadays and didn't need a man to survive. He could move to her town, find a job, then after he'd saved enough money, ask her to be his. After mating, they could go or do anything they wanted.

Fuck. He was so stupid. Why hadn't he thought of this earlier before screwing it all up? He glanced around wondering what was keeping his mate. He was about to step out of line to look for her when the cashier asked for the next person.

Considering how the female behind the counter fumbled with finding the bar code to scan on the food packets, she must've been new. When one refused to ring up, she pulled out a procedural manual and flipped through the pages.

Tevrik waited patiently. Juliet would be there any second. When she wasn't, his wolf started to pace. Something wasn't right. As soon as his items were bagged, he hurried toward the last place he saw her in the back by the refrigerated drinks.

She wasn't in the aisle anymore. In fact, she wasn't in any row. She was gone.

Calming himself, he took a deep breath. She wouldn't have walked out on him, would she? Granted his mate was pissed earlier, but she seemed to have forgotten about that with the discovery of the gold. She even said she'd meet him outside, that's it, she was at snowcat.

Juliet's smell was still strong though. So, where was she? He noted the scent carried to the side toward another row. There, he inhaled a new smell, and the blood in his veins froze. His mind put the scent to a person—Petey. The bastard had been talking to his mate.

He followed both fragrances through a side door into a warehouse space. From there, the trail diffused with the swirling air, but there was enough to lead him out the back door to a small area with several cars.

Eyes darting to each vehicle, he searched for the truck he saw in the diner parking lot with Frost. The one with the beat-up shovel that fell out of the back. He didn't see it. Why would he? If Petey was shopping, he'd be parked out front with the rest.

Racing back through the store, Tevrik dodged customers as he made his way to the double glass doors. The cashier scowled at him for causing such a ruckus. Once again, standing outside, he scanned the lot.

Would Juliet leave with Petey? Why? Did they know each other? And why would they leave out the warehouse exit?

He realized that he'd dropped the bag with Juliet's protein bars and juice. Confusion rumbling in his head, he went back inside to look for it. She might have asked Petey to take her to the airport if she was still really mad.

Through the overhead speakers, the cashier said, "Petey, please come up front for a price check."

How many Peteys were in this small town? Only one he knew of and he had his answer to his mate's disappearance. The rat bastard had taken her to get back at him for beating up on him and James the other day. Son of a bitch. He'd kill that mother fucker if he touched one hair on her head.

He spun around, his shirt tightening across his chest. Tevrik panted, straining to keep his wolf in check. Now wasn't the time to go feral. He needed his wits about him to find his mate.

He plowed through the entrance, slamming the door against the outer wall, shattering the glass. After climbing into his snowcat, he had to pull himself together to think clearly. Where was the most likely place Petey would go? His home. Tevrik was about to turn onto the main street when he realized he had no idea where Petey lived as an adult. Last place he knew was Petey's parents.

That would work. They would know where their cock-sucking son lived. He headed for the far side of town where the pack's subdivision stood. The location was created when his grandfather brought the group to civilization.

The pack built most of the homes themselves after watching a contractor build the first few. The town helped them put in streets and underground conduits for water and sewage. The division flourished when all the oil companies came drilling and laying pipe to transport oil to the States.

Except for those who owned a business—grocer, butcher, cinema, diner, etc.—the entire pack worked in the oil industry in one capacity or another—the men in the field and women in supporting roles. Even his mom and dad worked outside the house until running the large pack became a full-time job on its own.

His father was so proud of all they had accomplished in such a short amount of time. Leaving behind the old ways and fully embracing human tech-

'nology. He remembered the new playgrounds that had been installed in the park. Primary colors brightened the lush grassy area, the shiny metal slides with the required mud puddle at the bottom, and the merry-go-round that he pushed so fast in third grade that Melissa Carrington threw up.

The houses were always in pristine shape with white paint and quaint front porches resembling the perfect American home. Neighbors were constantly stopping by to say hello and invite the pups over to play. It was all such a far cry from where he had shacked up the last thirteen years.

As the sign for the community became visible up the road, his truck slowed. Or it could've been him not pressing the gas pedal quite as hard. Sweat broke out on his forehead. He contemplated turning around and going home until he remembered why he was here in the first place.

With renewed urgency and determination, he moved forward. Nothing was more important than Juliet. She was all that mattered. Not what the towns-folk or other shifters thought of him.

Wolf killer. Coward. Shit on the bottom of a shoe.

At the entrance, he noted the landscaping was only dirt with small piles of snow instead of the green plants he was accustomed to, but it was almost winter.

The wooden sign reading Wolf Grove could've used a coat of paint and a few nails to fix a broken board. He figured that would get done when it warmed.

But it didn't get any better after turning onto the one street running from entrance to exit. The initial houses on each side were owned by the Hadleys, older members of the pack. During his childhood, the homes had been kept up to make a great first impression.

But now, weeds had taken over the yards to the point the porches were hidden. Paint had peeled from the beams and siding, leaving a dead, ashy look to the once vibrant homes. The concrete walks leading from the street to the front doors had crumbled and disappeared into the dirt.

Tevrik couldn't believe what he saw. Had the owners died and no one bought the homes? Where were the grown children who were supposed to purchase their childhood homes to carry on the legacy with their own kids? Every other house was in the same rundown condition. And those that were lived in still looked in shambles. What had happened?

The school which should have had students and teachers and a lot full of cars was vacant, seemed abandoned. The playground equipment was rusted and falling apart. The butcher shop where old man

Tompkins kept massive freezers filled with beef and caribou was boarded up, some of the windows broken. The grocery was the same.

Tevrik turned the corner onto the street where Petey's parents lived. Scratched that. Had lived. The porch was destroyed, the column holding up the front gable broken and shingles littering the ground. The once-white picket fence was partially knocked over and the flower beds Petey's mother took pride in were sand pits where animals had taken their dumps.

He stopped and got out of the truck. He felt like he was in an episode of the Twilight Zone. Had the world gone to hell and left him behind?

A door opened across the street and he turned not knowing what to expect. Scouring his brain cells, he tried to recall who lived in the home.

"Hey, you," the woman hollered, "what do you want?"

"I was looking for Petey's parents," he replied.

The woman flipped her hand in the air. "They ain't been here for years." Wrinkling her nose, she stepped onto her porch. "Who are you, boy?" She sniffed. "You look familiar."

Panic raced through Tevrik. If someone recognized him, there'd be a witch hunt and a burning stake in his future. He dashed for the snowcat, hoping to get away before the lady figured out who he was.

He did a U-turn in the middle of the street and roared toward the main lanes. He zipped down to the old butcher shop and drove around back and parked. He puffed like he'd run ten miles.

Shit. That was a complete failure. So Petey's parents had been gone for a long time. That family was from the original pack. He would've thought for certain they would've stayed around no matter what.

Now what was he going to do? The more he contemplated the situation, the more he kept coming to one answer. He had to go home. He had to face his alpha, his father.

EIGHTEEN

J uliet woke with a headache from hell. The side of her skull felt ready to burst open and spew brains, which couldn't feel any worse. Her eyes saw walls made of logs, but this wasn't Tevrik's home.

A damp mustiness had settled in her nose, making her need to sneeze. If she did, her head would pop off like a zit. That could actually make her feel better. Instead, she pinched her nostrils, effectively relieving the itchiness until she breathed in again.

"Ah," a male voice said, "the princess is awake." Slowly, she rolled over, causing the coils of the bed she was on to squeak. Now, seeing the world around her, she remembered what happened. She'd been abducted again. This time it wasn't her fault though. Which pissed her off.

She snarled her lip. "You're goddamn right, the princess is awake. What the fuck is going on? I try to help you and you do this, you prick."

The men—Petey and another male—sat in front of a small fireplace, staring at each other, then at her. The other man broke into hysterical laughter. "Who the hell did you hijack?" He slapped his knee. "The Ice Queen herself?"

Petey growled. "Shut up, James. She's going to lead us to the gold."

Ah, of course. She'd mentioned the discovery a little too loudly, apparently, at the general store. Shit. The little hell hole they were in was cold. Air from outside virtually blew through the cracks in the casing around the window behind the bed.

The fire did little to warm the shack. Twigs and leaves littered the floor as if someone left the door open for a year and hadn't cared enough to sweep.

"Where are we?" she asked. "Take me back to town."

"Not yet, missy," Petey said, rising from his chair. "You're showing us where you found the stash." He leaned over a wobbly table with a map spread across it. A well-used map—frayed edges and holes abound.

Curious, she stepped up to the table and glanced down. In black ink, Xs and scratched out areas littered the paper which looked to be an illustration of the upper Alaskan mountain ranges.

"Are these the places you've searched?" she asked. Petey shoved her away with his hip.

"That's none of your goddamn business," Petey spit out. Not prepared for the physical aggression, Juliet stumbled back and lost her balance. Hands caught her before she slammed to the floor. She looked up into beady eyes. His hand slid up her torso to cover her breast.

Throwing an elbow, she tagged James in the jaw causing him to snap back. With his hand still wrapped around her arm, she couldn't get away from his retaliation—a fist to the face.

"Bitch," he yelled. Pain cascaded through her skull and neck. A wave of blackness tried to take her, but she fought it. Being unconscious wasn't cool with her. No telling what would happen to her body while she was out. She was sure it wouldn't be good.

Staying on her feet, she yanked her bicep from his grip. With a hand on the rough-hewn wall, she said, "I suggest you not touch me again."

Petey hacked out a phlegmy laugh. "We got ourselves a spirited mare, James. Leave her alone until we got the gold. Then we can do whatever we want."

James spun around. "Don't tell me what to do, asshole."

Juliet snorted. "Is that your encouragement for me to tell you?" She shuffled to one of the chairs in front of the fire. "Both of you are fucking idiots." She sat. "Wait till Tevrik finds us."

"Yeah," Petey said, "what are you doing with that stupid fuck? You're human."

A warning went off in her head. No wonder James didn't go down when she elbowed his face. These two were shifters, which changed things. She wouldn't be able to lie about anything. Shit. Instead of answering, she kept her mouth shut. James smacked her up the side of the head, nearly knocking her off the chair.

"You were asked a question, bitch," he said.

Blackness crept up on her vision again. She probably had a damn concussion by now. As soon as Tevrik got here, she would seek treatment, after she kicked this asshole's ass. When her previous abduction was over, she'd taken a series of self-defense classes. If she were smart, she would've taken them much earlier and may have been able to prevent her last situation.

The local police department offered the low-cost

programs that not only boosted her physical strength but gave her confidence to stand up for herself in the male-dominated lab. If she had her way, every female would learn what she did. With fewer easy victims, perhaps violence and other abuses would lessen. But against shifters, force wasn't going to work as well. She had to use her smarts.

And smart would be not letting her captors know her strengths. If they thought they had a scared human, then they would be less cautious with her. That could give her the opportunity to escape. She had to keep her eyes open for that moment.

She felt her hair moving. Before she could pull away, Petey jerked her out of the chair by her strands. He dragged her to the table and threw her against the edge.

"Point to where the gold is," he demanded.

She stared at the map. She had to stall to give Tevrik time. "I have no idea where it is on a map," which was a partial truth—this map looked nothing like the professionally printed plats she was used to —"I only know how to get there from town."

"Well, shit," Petey said.

James huffed. "I told you we should've stayed in town. I've hated this piece of shit hut since I was a kid."

"Yeah, well," Petey retorted, "burn it down, you whine baby." He threw James's coat at him. "Get the truck going. We're going into town then straight to the mountain." His eyes focused on Juliet as if saying she'd better play along or else.

NINETEEN

Tevrik couldn't put this off any longer; his mate depended on him. It had been fifteen years since he was there last. And in that time, something had happened to Wolf Grove to make it seem a rundown ghost town.

His wolf was just as nervous. They both knew they had failed. Failed the pup, the pack, and the alpha.

He stopped in the driveway beside the house. An old man with salt and pepper hair stood on the porch, dead center of the steps to the front yard. Tevrik couldn't decipher the look on his stoic face. Tevrik wondered which member of the pack he was.

Tevrik opened the truck door, stepped out, then

closed it behind him. He couldn't bring himself to move forward. The front door swung open and a small female flew out and shoved the man to the side. Next thing he knew, his back was plastered to the truck door, but the best smell in the entire world, next to his mate's, surrounded him. Mom.

She had her arms around him, bawling into his shirt. She mumbled words, but he couldn't make them out with her sobs. At least she wasn't yelling, telling him to never come back. Wolf killer.

He held his mother close, taking in more of her scent. God, he had missed her, not realizing how much until now. He fought the tears that threatened. Not cool to cry in front of the parents.

His mother pulled back and put her hands on his cheeks. "My baby wolf boy has grown up. You're taller than your father now."

He stared down at her face. Where there had been smooth skin around her eyes and mouth, wrinkles and creases had set in deeply. He supposed a lot of that had to do with him and his failure. But her smile was still as warm and welcoming as it had been.

"Where is Dad?" he asked. "I'm here to ask for your help. My mate's in trouble."

Her eyes widened. "You have a mate too?" She hugged him tightly again, another big sob tore from her chest. He didn't know how to take that. Was she happy or upset? He knew he didn't deserve to be happy, but he had found Juliet and wasn't giving her up. Fuck what everyone else thought.

The old man had stepped off the porch and wandered toward the two still against the truck. When he was closer, Tevrik fought a gasp. It was his father.

The alpha wolf had aged thirty years in fifteen. His white hair, normal for the arctic wolf, was a thin crown encircling his head. Streaks of steel gray high-lighted the narrow swath. The beard he sported was more black than white. His eyes drooped with heavy bags underneath as if the world had hung on them. Thick lines etched his forehead and the frown Tevrik had seldom seen him with.

With an arm still around his mother, Tevrik extended his hand to his father. Tevrik wouldn't have been surprised if his father rejected it. As expected, his dad ignored the customary greeting. Instead he stepped up to Tevrik and put his arms around his shoulders, squishing Mother in the process.

It wasn't the normal *slap on the back, how ya doing* hug. It was a *my missing son has come home* hug.

After a moment, his dad stepped back and slapped his shoulder. "Let's go inside, son—" his voice cracked on the last word as if he hadn't said it in a long time. His mother took his hand and they followed the old alpha into the house to the kitchen.

His home was as he remembered it, except with an updated and bigger TV in the living room. The blue sofa and matching loveseat hadn't weathered so well. The cushions sagged in the middle and the material was frayed in several places. His dad's leather recliner had an indention that perfectly outlined his father's form. Maybe it wasn't exactly how he remembered it. Why hadn't they purchased new furniture or updated the home? Something was wrong.

At the kitchen table, the two men sat and his mother pulled a can of his once favorite soup from the cabinet.

He didn't know where to begin. He had so many questions and he could tell his parents did too. But he had to find Juliet before Petey did something he'd regret.

Nobody said a word, waiting for the other to start. There was so much that had to be said. He released a deep breath.

"Dad, I need your help searching for my mate," he said.

"*Searching* for your mate?" his dad said.

Tevrik shook his head. Damn, had he forgotten

how to talk? "I mean, I have to get her back. I think Petey Mills took her to spite me."

"Hold on a second," his dad said, sitting back in his chair, "you've been here in town? For how long? Why didn't you come home?"

"No, Dad," Tevrik said, "it's not like that. I was. . .it's a long story and I have to find Juliet."

His mother set a bowl of the hot, chunky soup in front of him. "That's her name, Juliet? That's a lovely name."

"She's beautiful, actually," he said, staring at the bowl on the table. This soup he used to crave when he got home from school. He'd eaten several bowls of it a week. It was so delicious. But smelling it now, he wanted to throw it away. That wasn't how real tomatoes smelled, nor the meat. Acrid scents from the other vegetables stung his nose. Were those preservatives and chemicals used in making and canning the meal? Didn't his parents sniff that? Then again, why would they? He never did when all he ate came from the store.

"Thank you, Mom—"

His mother sat back, a tear in her eye. "You're welcome, son." She wiped at the tear. "You're so different."

His brows furrowed. "Different how?" He glanced from his mother to his father.

His dad smiled. "I've—we've—never heard 'thank you' come from your mouth."

Tevrik was ready to retort, but then realized they were right. Goddamn, he must've been so ungrateful as a child. He'd spent years blocking out everything that had happened before he left home for his own sanity.

He took his mother's hand from across the table and said, "I'm so sorry for all the stupid, idiotic things I said and did when I was a kid—"

His mom waved away the words, more tears gathering in her eyes. "We'll get to that stuff later. You said Petey Mills took Juliet and she is in danger." She looked at his dad. "You need to go to his home. Find that girl and teach that man a lesson, once and for all."

That didn't sound good. "What has Petey done to get a lesson from Dad?" He knew some of those lessons from his childhood and they weren't fun.

"Since his parents left, he's been a pain in the ass," his father said. "The boy can't keep his head out of his ass for one day."

Mom shooed them out the door. "Talk on the way there. I'll get the house ready." Tevrik was about to ask what she was getting the "house ready" for, but the front door closed. He thought he heard the word *grandpups*. Grandpups were on the agenda for his wolf? *Top of the list.* Tevrik had other ideas for the top of the list. Grandpups? Holy fuck.

No, no, no. Tevrik shook his head to clear those thoughts and focus on his father who was speaking and leading to the garage. "I'll drive since the SUV has more room."

Sliding into the front seat of the SUV, he realized that it would be just the two of them. He wasn't ready to talk to his father, to tell anyone, about where he'd been and endured for so long. He hadn't been able to get it out for himself yet. He waited in silence for his father to start the interrogation.

TWENTY

Tevrik sat in the passenger's seat of his father's SUV. It was just him and his dad, and the perfect environment to tear into him about everything that had happened.

Thinking back to that day, Tevrik figured the two wolves who were scouting with him had relayed the shooting and death to the family and the pack. He couldn't face the murdered boy's father or his own, so he ran. His dad probably knew the gist of what happened, but not the full story. The time had come to face the music.

"So," his dad started. Tevrik cringed inside, wondering which question would be first. "how long have you had your mate? A few years?"

That wasn't what he was expecting. Shock had him stumbling for words. "Uh, actually a few days."

"Days?" his father repeated.

"Yeah," he said, "she fell into my lap in an avalanche."

His father stomped on the brakes. "She what? An avalanche?"

Tevrik waved him on. "We'll tell you all that when we get her back. How far does Petey live from here?"

"Several blocks, but won't take long," his dad answered. Once again, seeing the devastation of the suburb, Tevrik has to ask. . .

"Dad, what's happened here? I mean, this is not the place it was fifteen years ago."

They turned the corner and his father let out a deep sigh. If it was possible to hang your head and drive, that was how his father looked. "I failed them, son."

"Failed who? What are you talking about? You're the alpha."

"Yes, and as the alpha, I've led the pack to its end. The pack is no more and it's because of me." Tevrik cranked sideways in his seat, speechless. He was the failure, not his father. His dad continued. "Not long after you left, the price of oil plummeted. The corporations that had employed almost everyone picked up their stuff and moved out of state. It had become too costly to drill up here.

"With them went the jobs, the money, and everything else it takes to make a living. Members couldn't afford to live here anymore. All the pups left to find jobs after school and never came back. The town of Antler can barely support the population it has now."

"But, Dad, that's not your fault," Tevrik burst out. "How could you know the businesses would leave?"

"That's just it," Dad replied. "I brought the pack into the modern age and we became dependent on humans and their ways of living. Now we don't know how to go on without money."

The SUV stopped and his father got out, headed for a house that needed to be condemned. Tevrik quickly caught up, barely holding back his need to rush forward and kill the bastard who took his mate. His dad put an arm out to keep him back.

"I'm the alpha still," he said. "Let me handle this." Tevrik nodded even though this was his mate they were here for and stepped back. His dad's fist hit the door hard enough that something inside crashed to the floor. Tevrik thought it was probably part of the roof.

When no answer came, his father backed away

and took in a deep breath through his nose. "His scent is weak. He hasn't been here for a while."

"He was working at the general store when we were there," Tevrik commented.

His dad looked at him with drawn brows. "You lost your mate at the general store? How old is she? Four?"

That was the father he knew. Sarcastic and the joke maker of the pack. Tevrik had lost track of the number of times his dad had embarrassed him in front of others with a dumb joke or something totally inappropriate—even if members laughed with him. He thought the kids were supposed to embarrass the parents.

"No, Dad," he growled, "she's not four. Come on." They shuffled through the snow back to the truck. After closing both doors, they sat quietly. "What now?"

His father cranked the engine. "He always hangs out with James Watson. Let's try his house." Tevrik remembered James from the diner parking lot. He and Petey were pieces of shit made for each other.

"Dad, what did you mean by Petey has been a pain in the ass?" Tevrik asked, thinking back to the conversation in the kitchen.

His dad let out another sigh as they turned a

corner. "In the past few years, we've had small robberies and thefts, cars broken into, that kind of stuff."

"And you think those two are responsible? Why don't their scents give them away?"

"They must've used some kind of scent blocker. The enforcers smelled only chemicals and the like from the blocker. No wolves."

Tevrik shook his head. So much had happened, had changed, in the time he was gone.

They parked on the street outside another shack that wouldn't pass any safety inspection. As they got out of the SUV, his father said, "When he's home, his truck is parked in the driveway." Tevrik picked up the tinge of gasoline in the air. James may have been there a while ago, but he'd recently fired up his truck and drove away.

Panic slowly made its way into his mind. He was so sure Juliet would be at one of their homes. Where else could they have taken her? His fists shook. If they hurt Juliet in any way, he would tear them limb from limb while they were alive. His wolf wanted out to hunt them, kill them.

"Get in the truck," his alpha ordered. The wolf had no choice but obey the order. Calming, Tevrik slid onto the seat and slammed the door closed. His panting fogged up the passenger-side window. "All right," his alpha said, "tell me all that happened when Juliet came up missing."

Tevrik threaded his fingers through his white hair and pulled. Anger, hate, and terror coursed through his blood making logical thinking almost impossible. All he wanted was to maim and kill.

"Tevrik Awulf," the alpha growled, "you will relax and recall what happened at the store. Now."

His wolf receded and Tevrik's breaths slowed. "Thanks, Dad. I've never had to deal with this kind of thing before. I don't know what to do."

His father's large hand gripped his shoulder. "You did good by coming to me. That's what pack is for." He was about to tell his father that he was wrong. Tevrik no longer belonged to the pack. He'd failed everyone long ago. "Now tell me about Juliet."

Those thoughts overshadowed all else.

"We stopped in at the store to get her food before I took her to the airstrip." His dad's brows raised, but he didn't interrupt. "We were kinda in a tiff and not talking at that moment." His dad smiled as if to say welcome to having a mate. "Then she yelled out for me and I came running to see her all aglow with excitement."

Tevrik twisted in his seat. "Dad, she found a stash

of gold. Huge nuggets like I've never seen in real life."

"You don't say?" he replied, hand smoothing down his beard. "Since you were in the store, you sure it wasn't the fake gold they sell? That shiny pyrite stuff."

"Oh, Jesus Christ, Dad. Now's not the time for joking around. She found the gold before the avalanche started on the *mountain*."

"Ah. Was she telling you this in the store?"

"Yeah," Tevrik replied. "I told her to keep quiet about it and we'd talk in the truck. I went to pay then couldn't find her after that. But I smelled Petey's stench mixed with my mate's scent."

Dad looked at him. "This might not mean much, but Petey and James are convinced Kitty Kalloway's lost gold is real. They've spent a lot of time in the mountains. I've had them watched for a while now to make sure they aren't causing trouble somewhere else when they aren't in town."

Tevrik was surprised to hear that tale's name. He'd told Frost about it not too long ago. "I guess that could be what Juliet found. I don't know how much is there. We hadn't gotten that far into the conversation."

"No, son," Dad replied, "that's not what I'm

getting at." He looked at his dad, wondering what the hell he had going in his brain. That was another reason he wasn't alpha material. He wasn't smart enough. "You know Petey works at the general store. He stocks shelves and unloads the trucks with merchandise," he paused for a moment.

"Fuck me," Tevrik shouted. "Petey heard Juliet talking. He could've been in the aisle over. The bastard took her to get to the gold she found, not to get back at me."

Dad nodded. "That's what I'm thinking."

"Son of a bitch." Tevrik hopped out of the SUV, stripping off his shirt then pants. "I'm going to the mountain."

"Which one," his father asked.

By giving the information to his father, Tevrik would be exposing where he had lived the past years. Was that something he wanted? His dad hadn't asked one question about anything but his mate. Hadn't said anything about the killing. Hadn't told him to get out and never show his face again. Maybe after all these years, his father forgave him.

"Crested Peak, about a half mile from the rockslide."

His dad nodded. "I know where that is—"

Tevrik slammed the door closed in his rush to

shift and run to his mate. The SUV started up and rolled down the deserted street toward the pack home. His wolf paced a moment for him to figure out the shortest way to get to the peak. He could go through town which would take several hours, or he could take the shortcut path to the tundra—his insides chilled at the memory—the path where it all happened fifteen years ago.

TWENTY-ONE

evrik stood in his wolf's form in the middle of the street of his hometown, unable to move. He knew the direction he had to take to get to his mate but he didn't want to go that way, couldn't go that way. He hadn't been there since that day. But for Juliet, he'd give his left testicle. His wolf shuddered at the thought and got moving.

He could do this. He would. His wolf broke into a run. They were wasting time whimpering like ninnies. The end of the houses came too quickly for him. The path began at the park. His wolf kept going even though he wanted to stop.

An alpha keeps his cool and thinks before he reacts. An alpha is strong with his emotions but still caring and empathetic. His father had taught him so much to prepare him to be leader. Out in the wilderness alone, alpha leadership was useless. But maybe what his dad showed him was for more than just leadership. Maybe he'd learned how to make it through life.

He reached the spot where he and his friends turned off to avoid the hunter. His wolf pressed on. That tree grew closer with every step he took. He wanted to do this in his human form, but his wolf repeated *mate* telling him Juliet came before the past because that's what it was—the past. Juliet was the future.

Regardless, the wolf paused at the base of the tree where he had found the young wolf bleeding out. He wanted to rant and rave and scream at the unfairness of life. Why take someone so young? What was the purpose? There was none. That's what hurt the most, knowing there was no reason, nothing came from the boy dying.

The saying *everything happens for a reason*— well, that was a bunch of bullshit. His wolf bowed his head to acknowledge the tragic loss, but that was it. If he wanted to continue to wallow in his own pity party as he had for the last decade, his wolf said he'd have to do it later. They were on a mission. Tevrik would find a way to memorialize the tragedy, to do all he could to make sure the boy was never forgotten.

Yes, Juliet was his mission. He couldn't provide

for her now, but he would find a way. He would not fail her as he had the others. Frost had asked him to carve out a few furniture pieces in the past which the dragon sold and he ended up with several hundred dollars. That much money lasted for years. He could use that skill to take care of his mate.

The shortcut across the tundra cut the time to get to Book Mountain in half compared to going through town. That road twisted and turned around a peak connected to Crested Peak. The tundra stopped at its base.

Reaching the cave that saved his life so long ago, he hurried through it, shifting into his human form. There on the ledge was the gap in the rock where his life was changed forever.

TWENTY-TWO

J uliet sat crushed between the pair of wolf shifters in the two-seat snowcat. The last couple of hours had been miserable. These guys smelled worse than dog breath.

She'd done what she could to stall as long as she could, hoping Tevrik would find her. With her senses about her now and in familiar territory, it looked like she'd have to save herself. How a little lady like her could escape shifter with super smelling and super-human speed, she had no clue.

The snowcat that she'd rented when she arrived sat exactly where she had left it. Snow had covered the tracks, but it looked ready to drive away.

James pulled a roll of duct tape from the floor between his feet. "Put your arms out," he ordered. She could only comply and watch as he wrapped the tape around her wrists. Well, that put a crimp in any escape plans.

"Where do we go from here?" Petey asked.

"We have to get out and walk the rest of the way," she answered. There wasn't any need to lie to them, they could smell it on her anyway. It was just gold. A boatload of gold. But not worth her life especially now with Tevrik in the picture.

On the journey here, it occurred to her that the reason Tevrik wanted her to leave was because he'd been alone for so long, that he didn't know how to be with someone else. Everything he did showed her how much he cared, how much he wanted to make her happy. That's not what someone who wanted you to go away did.

She'd take it slow with him. Raven always yelled at her for being so *in-your-face*. Get him used to being around another human, having someone in his space. Yes, that would be the plan. She could camp out in the company's cabin condo and visit him every day, every minute of every day. Every minute of the night sounded better. Her body heated remembering last night.

Both men in the snowcat looked at her, an evil glare from each. "What are you thinking about, princess?" James slid his hand up her thigh. "What-ever it is, it smells delicious."

Oh fuck. They smelled her getting hot for her mate. The thought of either these assholes touching her made her want to puke.

The truck stopped and the men climbed out, yanking her across the seat.

"Where to now, princess?" James flashed a razor-sharp claw in front of her face then placed it against her neck. "The truth the first time with no funny busi-ness is what we're wanting. If something doesn't go right, I'll slash your throat and leave you here to die."

The ass leaned back and breathed deeply. "Smell that fear floating off her, Petey. Doesn't that just crank up the ol' shaft." He reached between his legs and grabbed himself. Juliet looked away disgusted.

Petey grabbed a fistful of her hair and shoved her to her knees. He stepped closer and pushed her face into his crotch. "I'd say even more than that."

She'd had about enough of this shit. Her hands taped together, she made one big fist and thrust her arms upward as hard as she could. She hit her target and the dick fell back into the snow, hands cupped around his groin.

James laughed and grabbed her arm, lifting her to her

feet. He plastered his front side to her back. He nodded toward Petey. "You stupid fucker," James said, "you have to do it from the back like your wolf would. Then she can't do anything while you fuck her, dumb ass."

Oh, she was sure she'd find a way.

James pushed her forward. "Lead the way." He followed her to where the repelling gear was still attached to the rock. The avalanche hadn't touched this high up, just where she had been poking around.

"The cave is at the end of the rope. You'll have to dig for it if it's covered with snow. It's not that deep." James looked at her skeptically. She huffed. "Do you smell a lie anywhere?"

He stepped toward the rope. "Petey, get your ass over here and watch her. I'm going down to check it out."

The man lumbered up behind her. "Go, man. I'll take care of things up here."

James turned to him. "Keep it in your pants, asshole. After this, we can tie her up in the hunting shed to fuck whenever we want." He winked at her. "I'm looking forward to that."

Juliet watched as he took the rope and walked himself backward down the slope with no harness or other gear. He was going down using only his shifter strength. She wondered if there was a way to cut the rope. Within moments, she heard a whoop. How had he found it already? She'd hoped it would take a while, long enough for her to figure out a plan.

Shit. Now what?

TEVRIK PEEKED out of the hole in the cave where he'd come to meditate and thank the gods for their goodness and blessings. He saw James raking his clawed hand through the snow, searching for the opening, most likely.

When the man whooped, Tevrik pulled himself up through the hole and shifted into his wolf. The snow had been cold on his naked body, but his mind was set on search and destroy. He smelled Juliet. She was up top.

Crawling on his belly, his wolf blended in perfectly with the white powder around him. There was a reason arctic wolves were snow white.

As he approached the hole from below, he slowed. He wanted to make sure James wasn't standing at the entrance. Tevrik needed to be inside to take out the bastard. Or he'd just wing it. Sticking his nose into the opening, he smelled James was deeper in the cave. He crawled in, then shifted into human form.

Like all shifters, he was able to see in the near darkness. With the cave being soundless, hearing where James stood was effortless. Tevrik slid along the wall, wanting to sneak up on him. Coming to a bend in the rock wall, he paused, not able to see around.

Suddenly his instincts told him to dive for the floor. As he went down, a rusty pickax swung around the corner and embedded in the rock where his head had been. Tevrik rolled to his feet, coming up to face James.

"What are you doing here, wolf killer?" James said, a hint of surprise in his voice. Then he smiled. "Petey said the princess and you were talking in the store, but he didn't say you were sweet on the little thing. Too bad we've decided to keep her around. Her pussy smells too good to let go." He laughed at Tevrik's expression.

Tevrik was barely holding it together. His wolf didn't want to kill now. It wanted to disembowel and leave the fucker for the bugs.

James pulled out a gun. "Now, don't get any ideas there, baby killer. We don't want anyone getting hurt."

He snorted. "Really? A shifter with a gun? Isn't

that a bit cowardly, James? Not depending on your wolf to protect you? How pathetic is that?"

The dickwad thrust the weapon toward him. "Shut the fuck up. My wolf is as strong as an alpha. Stronger, in fact."

That was interesting, he thought. Why bring up the alpha if not wanting the position?

Tevrik smirked. "So, you're planning on taking over the pack then?"

"Your father has done nothing but run it into the ground."

"The reason is because the oil companies went away," Tevrik clarified, defending his dad. "How do you think you're going to run the pack then?"

James's smile widened. "Why, look at all this gold." Behind the asshole, Tevrik noted a chest and several bags on the ground. "I'd say a million, wouldn't you?"

It clicked then. "You're going to bribe the pack into making you the alpha?" Tevrik said. "You're dumber than I thought. Why don't you crawl back into the hole you came from?"

James didn't seem to like his reply. He raised the gun, pointing it at his head, and fired. Tevrik dove to the side, but with little space to move in, that wasn't far enough. The bullet slammed into his shoulder. He fell backward, stumbling to the ground. James stepped toward him, gun in his outstretched hand.

"Some human inventions outdo claws," James smirked. "Looks like the pack has two wolf killers now." He raised the weapon again.

Tevrik had nowhere to go to avoid the fatal shot to his head. But under his hand rested a fist-sized rock. If his aim was true and the timing perfect, maybe he'd walk out of here. He studied James's hand holding the gun. As the forearm muscles tightened to squeeze the trigger, Tevrik hurled the rock at the muzzle.

When speeding metal smashed into rock, the stone exploded, particles spewing in all directions. The stunt startled James enough for Tevrik to dive forward to tackle the man. But James twisted away, stepped on the pickaxe, losing his balance. He went down with a sickening thud of his skull against the cave wall.

Tevrik knew instantly that James was dead. Even though a moron, he didn't need to die. Tevrik felt sorrow at the loss of life, but he wasn't going to dwell on it. His mate wasn't in his arms yet.

TWENTY-THREE

After James had been gone several minutes, Petey turned to Juliet and raked his eyes down her body. Seriously, she was going to throw up.

If he stepped closer, her boot would go someplace that was already tender on him. "Stay away from me, prick," she said, backing.

His eyes lit, probably from smelling her fear. Seemed she needed to do something about that. Pulling confidence from her self-defense training, she stood straighter and felt calm roll through her. She might take a beating, but she could give as well as she took. Petey stopped in his tracks. A frown marring his ugly face.

"I'm going to wait in the truck." She backed around the front of the snowcat. He grunted at her but stayed where he was closer to the edge. They both knew he had the key in his pocket, so she wasn't going anywhere.

What he didn't know was that she never took the key out of the ATV she drove up here.

A sound like a muffled gunshot resounded through the air. Petey turned to look over the side. "What the fuck? James," he yelled. "James, you okay?"

This was it. With Petey's attention elsewhere, she ran for her all-terrain vehicle. Her taped hands weren't helping any, but she'd work around them. She yanked the door open, slid inside and locked it. The sound of the engine sputtering had Petey turning around.

"Come on, come on," she prayed, hoping the damn thing would start before he reached her. She turned the key again, but the engine didn't catch. It had been sitting in the cold too long.

Just before Petey got to her, she gave up on the key and slid onto the passenger seat. When Petey's beefy arm came through the side window, she plastered herself to the far door. His alligator arms didn't reach her. Then he wised up and stepped back to open the door.

Juliet pulled on the latch and fell backward into

the snow. Again, with her hands tied, she had trouble getting up. Roaring like a beast, Petey dove over both seats of the small vehicle and grabbed her ankle.

She delivered the toe of her boot to the bottom of his chin. His head snapped back and she was able to get away. But now what? Running was her only option, and it wasn't a good one. Before she gone more than a few feet, she felt a hand grasp the back of her coat and jerk her back. She lost her balance, but he continued to drag her back to the ATV.

When they reached the guys' snowcat, Petey grinned down at her then tightened his grip and launched her into the air to slam against the side of the truck. Her head smacked the hard surface, dizziness making her collapse. He lifted her by the arms and hooked her bound wrists on a latch that held skis to the top of the vehicle. Her toes skimmed the snow.

Shoving her legs apart, he scooted forward against her, killing any hope she had of kicking him. There were other ways to fight back, and she would once the world stopped spinning.

He unzipped her coat and squeezed her breasts. She wiggled and thrust against him. Desperate to get him away, she dug the heel of her shoe into his thigh. He yelled out then slapped her cheek, wrenching her head to the side. Blackness was quickly eating away the scene.

No. She fought to stay alert as his hands fumbled with the button on her pants. What the fuck did he think he was going to do? It was below freezing. Didn't he know what happened to dinkies when it was cold?

In a blink, he jerked away from her and his body slammed, twice, against the side of the snowcat like she had earlier. Then Tevrik growled as he threw the dickwad *over* the roof to the other side.

"Juliet," he said, studying the hook her hands were attached to, "are you hurt?" Carefully, he lifted her, freed her from the latch, and put her on her feet.

"I'm okay except for my head. I'm too dizzy to stand. Wait. How did you find me? How did you know—"

Another gunshot went off, this time ringing her ears. Tevrik disappeared from her view and she started to slide down the vehicle's side.

"Come on, bitch." Petey grabbed her and tossed her over his shoulder. There, she saw Tevrik lying in the snow. Two things she noticed right away. One, he was naked. Two, blood was spilling onto his chest from the bullet wound.

She screamed his name or at least thought she did. With the ringing in her ears, she couldn't hear anything. Petey dumped her head first on the passenger side of the truck. Her head in the footwell, her legs were free to kick as hard as they could. And she laid into him as he drove.

He smashed his fist against her shinbone, sending a numbness to her toes. He grabbed her other ankle and pinned both her legs between the seats. In that position, she was stuck—still unable to use her hands. Goddamnit, that pissed her off. Using her teeth, she started tearing away at the tape. Enough of this shit.

From the corner of her eye, she saw movement at the driver's side window. Tevrik, except for the blood covering him, ran alongside the vehicle. Wolves were fast and snowcats were slow. Great combination as far as she was concerned at the moment.

The side glass shattered and her mate reached in, wrapping his hand around Petey's throat. Instead of releasing her legs, the dickhead took his hand off the wheel to punch and scratch at Tevrik.

She tried to pull herself into the seat but had nothing to hold onto. Fuck, this was so not good. At least her hearing was coming back. She heard Tevrik yelling at her.

"Juliet, get out!"

No shit, she wanted to tell him. What did he think she was doing? Enjoying the view from down there?

"Now, Juliet," he continued as he fought Petey to grab the steering wheel. "There's a cliff."

TWENTY-FOUR

Tevrik lay in the snow, a second bullet in his body in as many minutes. The son of a bitch shot him. What a wuss. What happened to a good ol' challenge to the death? Claws versus claws. Teeth versus teeth.

After James had fatally hit his head, in Tevrik's human form, he climbed the hundred feet to the peak. The rope was quite helpful in making that task fast. Standing on the rocks, he looked around for Petey and his mate. He didn't see either but saw the snowcat in front of him shimmy and heard a crash against the side. He raced around and found his mate hanging from a bar on the roof and Petey with his hands unfastening her pants.

Fury like he'd never felt ripped through him. Tevrik reached to tear the bastard's head off, but he moved and Tevrik got a handful of jacket. With that, he slammed Petey's body into the already dented side and then threw him over the vehicle, but that wasn't nearly enough to satisfy his thirst for the man's blood.

A whimper from Juliet instantly quieted his animal. He got her to her feet, then the asshole came around the front of the snowcat with a hunting rifle in hand. He must've pulled it from inside the truck. Tevrik should've known—if James had a gun, so would his dumb fuck buddy.

The pain in his chest radiated like lightning burning through him. He needed to shift to heal the wound, but unlike James's shot which exited Tevrik's body, the rifle's bullet didn't. Shifting wouldn't do much but stop the external bleeding. He could still bleed to death internally if he didn't get help quickly. That was nice and all, but he had more important things to take care of. His mate.

Borrowing speed and strength from his wolf, he took off after the truck with his mate and Petey inside. Fortunately, vehicles with tank tracks didn't move as quickly as a wolf shifter. He caught up fast. Petey drove over the ridge where there was no place to go. What the fuck was he thinking? Or was he?

The wild look in the man's eye sent terror through Tevrik. This was a man not in his right mind. A man who didn't think logically about what he was doing.

A man willing to accept death as the end game. Petey took his hand off the wheel and stared into Tevrik's eyes. Petey knew as well as Tevrik that the ridge ended in a cliff. The bastard was trying to take both Juliet and Tevrik over the edge with him.

Tevrik yelled at Juliet to get out of the truck. He didn't know why she was on the floor. He couldn't see fully inside. Just enough to know she wasn't making progress toward the door.

He tried to grab the wheel to steer away from the looming drop, but Petey blocked access.

"Juliet, get out. Get out—" He was shoved away from the snowcat as it tipped forward, the front end dipping, then succumbed to gravity, falling over the edge out of sight..

His mate wasn't on the ridge. She had gone over, trapped in the snow vehicle.

Deep laughing turned his head. Petey's fucking face looked at him from where he climbed over the ledge. Smile on the dickhead's lips.

"Sorry, man," the bastard said, "was that your girl-friend?" He chuckled and crawled farther in and sat. "Whew. Was that a rush or what?"

Tevrik was in a daze. There, a waste of a wolf sat, and his mate was gone. Sweet, loving, Juliet gone. An explosion far away made him cringe. An image of his beautiful mate as a burned skeleton flashed in his mind. Both he and his wolf cried out an agonizing howl that resonated from the depths of his soul.

Tevrik's breathing picked up, getting shallower. "You killed my mate. The only woman I have and will ever love." He stalked toward Petey.

The asshole lumbered to his feet. "How about you join her, then. I won't mess it up this time."

Tevrik stopped in his tracks. "Mess up what?"

Petey laughed and took his shirt off. "You kill James? I was so tired of him trying to be in control."

"I didn't have a choice, Petey," Tevrik said. "I don't go around killing needlessly."

The big wolf shrugged. "I would've killed him if you hadn't. Wouldn't be my first."

Shock rolled through Tevrik. Petey acted as if murder was nothing. Who had he killed? This man in front of Tevrik wasn't the boy he knew years ago. A cruel hardness had set in him.

"Really," Tevrik said, playing along, "who have you killed lately?" Hopefully, the idiot would bite and brag about all he'd done.

Petey laughed again. "Nobody you'd know, except for one, a long time ago." He toed off his boots. Tevrik thought back in time. There was only one person he knew who was killed. The Brinkley boy there on the path in the woods. The one he had failed to protect those many years back. His mind stuttered at the revelation. Petey had shot the boy. Not a random hunter?

Tevrik stepped farther away from the cliff's edge, ready for Petey's shift. This would no doubt be a fight to the death. "Why would you shoot a kid? What did he do to you?"

Petey shrugged. "Not my idea. James thought if you were out of the way, then he and I could challenge your father for the pack."

That threw him for a loop. "Hold on, Petey." He held his hands out to stop any fight. This was beyond crazy. "You're telling me as a senior in high school, you thought you could take over and run a pack? You? A kid without a diploma yet?"

Petey's face reddened and his hands balled into fists. "I was the biggest after you. If things had gone as planned, I would be alpha and everyone would be worshipping me."

"First off," Tevrik said, "the alpha isn't a worship position. It's respect and trust, you dumb ass. And what was this plan?"

Petey stepped closer and Tevrik sidestepped in a circular direction. He needed to keep Petey talking if he was going to get what the dickwad knew. It seemed he'd misjudged the two misfits from school. They were missing more marbles than he thought.

Petey smiled. "I really shouldn't tell you. James would be pissed off."

"But James is dead, remember. You don't have to do anything he says anymore." Tevrik played to the man's ego. "You're your own wolf. Man up and let the world know how smart you are. The plan failed because it was James's, right?"

"Damn right it was," Petey spit out. "He thought if we used scent blocker, you wouldn't know we were there. Then when you were close enough, I'd shoot you in the head!" Petey let out a whoop. Apparently, he thought it funny that he had killed the Brinkley boy. Was that what Petey had said in his convoluted way?

Fuck. This was completely out of hand. Had he hit his head on a rock and was dreaming up this shit? Even he wasn't this creative.

They circled each other, both men naked. The bullet wound under his collarbone started to ache. With all the adrenaline racing through him, his body had been numb to the injury and the cold. Now that was starting to fade. He could feel his legs weakening.

Petey sniffed the air and smiled. "It's about time. I

knew if I kept you talking, you'd bleed out enough for me to bash your head into the rocks."

Wait, what? Petey kept him talking? Tevrik thought it was the other way around. Who was playing whom? Petey leapt toward him, shifting midair. Tevrik rolled to the side, shifting as he sprang to his four feet.

Petey was a big wolf, larger than he'd been in school. And so was he, but he'd had don't anything close to fighting. They were way out of practice in the ways of battle.

Petey's timberwolf colors contrasted with Tevrik's all white. One was common while the other rare. Both jumped and they slammed chests, claws slashing. Each landed on their feet, but the bullet in Tevrik ripped through more muscle, painting his pristine coat bright red.

They bit at each other, coming away with mouthfuls of fur. Petey swiped at his head. Tevrik wasn't fast enough to dodge and he flipped onto his side, waiting for the spinning to stop. With his loss of blood, Tevrik found it difficult to get to his feet.

Wobbly, he stood on all fours, his eyesight wavering between single and double vision. Petey charged him, shoving him backward in the snow.

Tevrik forced himself to his feet, only to have Petey push him farther back.

As he lay, exhausted, on his side, panting for breath, he saw Petey's plan. Tevrik's head was a yard from the edge of the peak. One more ram and he'd slide over the side to join Juliet at the bottom. That idea sounded fine to him. What was his life without Juliet by his side? He'd be back to the way things had been the past fifteen years. He couldn't do that, not after experiencing life with his mate.

Then he saw his mom and dad running toward him. Their snow truck was parked behind the others. He wondered how long they had been there. Had they heard Petey's confession? His mom yelled for him to get up as she got closer.

He was so tired and felt so cold. His thick coat should've kept the chill away, but death crept along his bones. It was welcome if it took him to his mate. Then he heard a growl and his mother slid to a stop, staring at Petey.

That son of a bitch. How dare that dickhead bare his teeth at his mother. No one threatened his family while he was around.

Tevrik rose to his feet, lips pulled back, ready to attack if Petey so much as leaned toward his mother. Seeing him up, Petey focused on him again.

Stretching back, Tevrik's hind paw felt the edge of the cliff. He was closer than he thought. Petey tore through the snow toward Tevrik. The only place to go was over the side. So, Tevrik shifted to his human form, falling to one knee from the exertion it took to change. His blood painted the snow in splotches.

He braced for impact from the big wolf. With open maul and teeth flying toward him, Tevrik reached out and grabbed onto fur. He rolled backward, using the wolf's momentum to sling the animal above his head and over the side. That should've been it, but it wasn't.

While Tevrik thought he'd grabbed onto the wolf's facial fur, it turned out that Petey had one of Tevrik's hands between his teeth. When Tevrik released the animal to fly over the cliff, Petey held onto the hand, pulling Tevrik with him.

Just like in the movies, time seemed to slow. He stared into the hate-filled eyes of the madman/wolf. If he could've seen Petey's human face, he was sure the man would've been smiling, thinking he had won. He had finally bested the alpha's son.

Tevrik snorted. Not happening.

With his free hand, he reached out to grab onto something, quickly realizing there was nothing but rocky surfaces. Maybe it was happening.

Then to his shock, as he went over, a small hand snapped out and grabbed his outstretched arm. The hand yanked him hard toward the rocks. His fingers in the animal's mouth slid free and he wrapped them around a protrusion below a pair of boots he recognized from when he took them off his mate.

Tevrik's body slammed against the cliff side, but now he had a reason to hang on. The most beautiful face he'd ever seen looked down on him. Her feet rested on a slab of cracked stone, secure and relatively safe.

So much joy rushed through him, he almost let go of the rock he was holding. She eyed his body, stretched out and naked. When she licked her lips, he scowled, and of course, his dick hardened.

"Juliet, stop that. My parents are here."

TWENTY-FIVE

After helping Tevrik's mother dig the bullet out of her son's chest, then his subsequent shift and healing, Juliet and the three shifters sat around the fire in Tevrik's small cabin, sipping hot herbal tea and munching on fresh fruit from the greenhouse. Hours had passed as Tevrik told his parents about his sojourn and how he'd been living in this cabin over the years.

"I must say, Tevrik," his mom said, "this tea is better than anything you can buy at the store." She glanced toward the door leading to the greenhouse. "And this fruit is fabulous. You've been growing your own food all this time?"

He nodded. "Once it's all set up, it's not hard to maintain." He rocked back and forth and gently rubbed a hand down Juliet's side. She leaned against him in the chair.

He gave her a semi-fake snarl. "And you," he said, tightening his arms around her waist, "why didn't you tell me you knew about shifters? Do you have any idea what I was going through trying not to expose myself?"

She giggled. Her man, wolf, was so adorable. "How was I supposed to know that you didn't know that I knew shifters existed?"

He stared at her for a second, shook his head, then asked, "How are the ribs feeling?"

"Better," she answered. "It's really just the one side I landed on that hurts."

Dad cleared his throat. "How did you get down the side of the cliff in the first place?"

She looked at Tevrik and his expression was as questioning as his father. Her mate asked, "How did you get out? I thought you were d—gone." She felt his heart stutter on the word he couldn't voice. Dead.

She rested her mug on her lap. "It all happened so quickly. I tried to find something to hold onto to pull myself onto the seat. The only thing I could grab was the latch to the door. When I did, the door popped open and I was able to grab the seat and scramble out. Actually, it was more like the truck fell away from me as I reached for the cliffside. Either way, I was very fortunate to have stopped sliding after a few feet."

Tevrik squeezed her, getting a yelp from both of them. Her for her sore ribs, and Tevrik for using his injured arm. After a short laugh, the room quieted. Juliet wondered why everyone wasn't hugging and kissing and bundled around each other after being separated for so long. Well, if no one else was going to talk, then she would.

"Tevrik, I heard you talking with Petey after the snowcat went over the cliff. What was that all about? Did Petey say he killed people? He was, like, bragging about it." Tevrik's face paled and she glanced between him and his parents. "Should I not have asked that?"

Dad said, "Your mother and I heard most of what he said." He was about to say more but didn't.

Juliet studied her mate. She smiled remembering what he said to Petey—she was his mate and he loved her. She knew he did. His actions proved it. The big turd was just too scared to say it. Typical.

She hugged on him and said, "It's okay to tell, babe. We all love you here." She had a feeling that what needed to be said was the root of all the isolation and loneliness on Tevrik's part. Something he hadn't even told her yet.

"Yeah, all right." He snuggled her closer and stopped rocking. After a deep breath, he started. "It was time to check the northern perimeter like we always did the last Saturday of every month. When I, Tony, and Devon got to the park, the Brinkley boy was there. He wanted to go with us and I told him no because it was a long trek and could be dangerous for someone not strong enough.

"He mouthed off that he was strong enough, but at ten years old, he was still just a pup. We weren't much older in reality but at that age, you couldn't tell us we were too young. The stupidity of teenagers you know. Anyway, I told him to go home and we watched as he stomped across the playground. In our wolves, we went on down the shortcut to the tundra, like normal.

"About halfway through, my wolf smelled something strange. It wasn't a natural nature smell. It stung my nose like a chemical or something. The other guys didn't smell it, but I took us off the trail and through the woods anyway."

At that moment, some of Petey's ramblings started to make sense to her. Juliet said, "Petey said James had them use scent blocker so you wouldn't know they were there. Then they planned on shooting you. But you smelled the block and changed course, right?"

He nodded. By his shell-shocked expression, she

saw the pieces fall into place in his mind also. He asked, "But why would he shoot the kid?"

Juliet replied. "Because he thought it was you. Either he didn't wait to make sure or the boy could've been sneaking through the trees along the path so you wouldn't look back and see him. When noticing light colored fur, Petey shot at it."

Tevrik dropped his forehead onto her shoulder. She felt his mental anguish of reliving that event. He'd probably spent the last decade of his life trying to forget it.

His mom's voice floated to Juliet softly. "Why did you run, Tevrik? Why not come home. It wasn't your fault."

His head popped up. "But it was, Mom. Don't you see that? I should've known what that smell was. I should've known the kid would follow us. An alpha protects the pack, keeps them safe. And I failed: failed to protect the boy, failed to protect my pack, and failed you. I didn't deserve to be alpha. I blamed myself and that was all I could think about. I was too ashamed."

Juliet raised a hand, stopping the argument before it started. "Tevrik, finish your story, then we'll decide how dumb it was for you to run."

He kissed her cheek and continued. "After hearing

the gunshot, I ran back and smelled blood. I trailed the scent to the small wolf's body lying against a tree. He looked like he was just sleeping, his head propped up on a root. I was going to yell at him for putting himself in danger. There was a hunter nearby and he could get hurt." He shook his head, shaking the memory off.

"Then I saw the blood run from under his body like a creek through a deep valley. I knew what happened. I knew I had failed him, failed the pack, failed as an alpha. I-I couldn't face you all and see the disappointment, knowing I let you down as the next alpha."

Juliet held him, giving him her love and support. Her heart ached over the tragedy, over how he felt.

"Tevrik," his father said, "you are not a god. You can't know everything—"

"But you always do," Tevrik barked. "You are the perfect alpha."

"Perfect?" his father repeated. "Did the pack look *perfect* when you were there? Did all the closed shops and boarded up houses look *perfect* to you?"

"Dad," Tevrik huffed. "That's not what I mean. You know everything, how to take care of every situation, always make the best decision. I would never be worthy of such a position. I couldn't even keep a child safe."

His father leaned forward "You were a child yourself. No one would have blamed you. The whole pack mourned both of you. Even the other two with you, Tony and Devin, knew the truth of the incident. They were so upset about losing you, they left the pack after graduation, never coming back."

Juliet leaned forward and set her mug on a stump acting as a side table. Then she turned in the chair and took his face in her hands, letting her own alpha rise to the surface. "Now, listen up, pup. I don't want to hear anything like that come out of your mouth again. You are more than worthy of being an alpha." He shook his head.

She continued. "Yes, you are. You saved my life at least twice, and found those traps before I stepped on one, kept me from walking into a den of wolves—"

"Yeah," he butted in, "then you almost fell off the mountain to your death." His parents gasped.

Juliet ignored it. "And you saved me. Do you think I would've made it to the rock path on my own? What's one of the most important things for an alpha besides safety?" When he didn't say anything, she went on what Raven told her. "To feed your mate and the pack. My god, Tevrik, you have a grocery store of fresh produce outside your door. If I wanted a steak, I'm sure you have a few hiding around here somewhere.

"And you healed me, Tevrik. I could barely breathe and sure I was going to die, but you knew what was wrong and you fixed it. I was almost normal the next morning. Maybe not right now, but we'll take care of that later." She gave him a wink, hoping to lighten the sting of her words.

"You nursed me back to health. You showed me the beauty of nature with the cubs and sunset. You appreciate all the world has to offer. What more could a great alpha possibly do that you haven't shown me you're capable of?"

His mom cleared her throat. "There's that pesky matter of grandpups. Plural."

Tevrik dropped his forehead against hers. "Please tell me my mother didn't say that out loud."

Juliet placed a quick peck on his lips. "Plural," she said with a smile.

TWENTY-SIX

After several hours, Tevrik's parents left with a promise to come back later the next day, Juliet lay spooned into her mate's body. She could get used to these super long nights. As long as they were in bed together the whole time.

With no TV, internet, radio, neighbors, or anything else to steal her mind, she thought back through the day. It had started so well, then got crappy, then really crappy, then great, and now was perfect. But one question plagued her.

"Babe," she said. She got a lazy *hmmm* for an answer. "What did your father mean when he said that the pack didn't look perfect nor were the closed shops were perfect?"

He sighed and propped his head up on his elbow. "Well, with the price of oil being so low over the years, the businesses in Alaska moved to other places.

So the pack members had to leave the pack community to find work. Most moved to the cities, leaving the community here almost vacant."

"Oh," she replied, "that's it?"

A frown marred his face. "What do you mean by that? It is a big deal."

She rolled over to see him. "Why not just move the pack to a new location outside the city where most of them are?" Duh? His eyes widened. That idea appeared to be new to him. Did the man not know how to pack up and live someplace different? After she thought about it, the answer was probably no.

"And," she continued, "build the community so they aren't so dependent on money or what the humans do. Every home should have their own greenhouse, fireplaces and rock walls, all the stuff you have here." Then a thought hit her. "Well, maybe running water for the bathroom would really be more sanitary."

He laughed. "What? You don't like packing snow into the tank every time?" He brushed his hand over the covers, scooting her body into his. His deliciously long and hard cock pressed into her thigh. "And where would the pack come up with all this money needed to 'just move the pack to a new location'?"

Getting into the game, she wet her finger and

slowly dragged it around his nipple, making it taut. "I just happen to know where a million dollars is lying around."

His face turned serious. "Legally, that's your money. Finders keepers."

"No," she replied, "it's *our* money. And with you as the new pack alpha, it should be used for the pack."

"But—"

She put a finger over his lips. "Butts are for spanking. And yours will be next if we don't get working on your mother's one request."

He smiled. "Plural." He leaned forward and kissed her. "I will never tire of looking at your gorgeous body."

She licked her lips, the taste of him bursting to life on her tongue. His head came down, his lips attached to the base of her throat. Electric tingles raced to her pussy. She raked her nails into his hair, pressing him to her chest as he glided to her breast.

"You smell so fucking good," he growled into her breast. The vibration from his rumble added to the desperation tensing her muscles.

"Tevrik, please," she finally choked out. The words traveled up her sandy throat to come out a bare whisper on her dry lips.

He glanced up and met her gaze. "I plan to please you, sweetheart."

One moment he was getting on his knees and the next his tongue was flicking mercilessly over her clit. A short breathless moan struggled out of her throat. Her legs started shaking, but he didn't stop. He pressed into her sex, his tongue lapping at her clit and dipping into her channel to fuck her in quick drives.

"Oh, my god. Oh my god!"

Her hips bucked forward. He lifted one of her legs and placed it over his shoulder. She let go of his hair and grabbed the sheet to cling to. Then he cupped her ass and lifted her, giving her the ability to place her other leg over his shoulder and bring her body off the bed.

He licked her with purpose, his growls and snarls making her more than a little crazy.

Tevrik's tongue flickered in quick circles over her hard clit. Her pleasure center ached with her need to come.

"Jesus, Tevrik, make me come already," she groaned.

He chuckled into her pussy, the vibration sending her so close to the edge, she took a sharp breath.

His licks on her clit increased, followed by sucking motions and the grazing of his teeth. Good god! She would argue with anyone that those were the easiest ways to make a woman lose her mind. She flew. Her back bowed and she dug her nails into the bed at the same moment her channel contracted around his tongue. Fucking hell, he was good at that.

Her knees were still shaking and her breaths coming in short gasps when he slowly and so carefully placed her legs on the mattress. She kissed him hard, licking her own body's juices off his lips and getting wet all over again. His hands caressed her full body, branding every bit of her flesh as his own. She was his and they both knew it.

He turned her over, she held onto the bed frame with shaky hands, she pushed her ass out and leaned forward, curving her back and offering her backside to her mate.

A soft growl sounded from behind. She heard his need in his breathing, sensed it in the tension floating over her back. He was close to losing control of his human body and letting his animal take control.

She gave a loud gasp when his tongue trailed from her ass up her spine to her neck. He slammed a hand on the bed, his fingers turned to claws. Oh, yes. He was very close to losing it.

"Juliet…"

She licked her lips and held her breath, waiting

and wanting. Lord, she wanted him more than her next heartbeat. More than knowing there would be a tomorrow. She wanted to hold on to that moment and freeze it in time. One breath. Two breaths.

He slid his cock between her pussy lips, using her body's moisture as lubricant. "You're so fucking wet, baby."

She gripped the bed, her body practically vibrating with need. If he didn't get on with it soon, she might disintegrate into nothing. "Do you like it?"

She knew better than to ask. He reeled back and one of his hands slapped onto her hip, digging his claws into her flesh. The bite of pain felt fucking amazing. Then he pushed forward, his cock fully embedding inside her, hot and hard, like steel on fire. She squeaked, almost slamming into the bed only to be hauled back into his body.

"I don't like it. I fucking love it. Your," he snarled the words by her ear, "slick little pussy is all mine, baby girl." He licked her shoulder. A shudder raced up her spine. He propelled back and thrust hard, holding her in place so she wouldn't slam into the headboard.

"Fuck me!" she moaned. It wasn't her telling him, it was an expression of how torn she felt over how he drove her slowly insane.

"Do you feel that, sweetheart?" He bit on her earlobe and sucked. "Feel my cock taking what's mine?" He bit her. "Do you?"

She nodded.

"You. Are. Mine."

She gulped and continued driving back into each of his plunges. Tension curled around her belly into a tight knot. "Tevrik, I--"

"I'm not stopping. Not until your pussy is wrapped tightly around my cock and you're left shaking from how hard you come. And trust me, sweetheart, you will come that hard."

Oh, she knew that was a definite. She mumbled under her breath about him taking too long.

"You want to come, baby. I know you do." He increased the speed of his thrusts. "You want my dick deep and far. As far as I can get. You want my mate stamp on you from the inside." He took a rough breath. "You want me to give you pups." He nibbled on her shoulder. "I want them too."

His hand curled around her belly, sliding between her legs to play with her clit. She mewled, wiggling back into his harsh drives. More. More. More. She was so fucking close.

All it took was a few flicks of his finger on her aching pleasure center in combination with his deep plunges and she was gone. The orgasm tore through her like a category five hurricane. It left her breathless, shaking and ready to fall apart. Only with Tevrik could she open up enough to lose herself in how he made her feel.

She was still riding the wave when he pressed tightly into her, his cock pulsing inside. He came with a loud howl.

EPILOGUE

Juliet stood outside the construction site trailer and sucked in a deep breath. Damn, she loved it here, and Alaska in the middle of summer was awesome. Temps averaged around seventy, and there were nineteen hours of daylight. Which was bad for baby production, but good for building a new community. Besides, baby production was well under way. She felt like an elephant carrying quadruplets. Her mother-in-law told her that was normal for shifter babies.

She surveyed the street with the second row of pack houses going up. The crews worked fervently to get up the fifty houses before winter weather hit. As news spread to distant pack members about the relocation, over half wanted to move in as soon as possible. Fairbanks, Alaska, wasn't the largest city, but it didn't have the traffic congestion of larger places while still providing work opportunities.

From a semi-tractor trailer, men offloaded green-tinted panels to set up the next series of greenhouses. Solar panels were being unpacked for installation. Energy conservation technology she didn't even know existed wowed her. But she was also thrilled with the old-fashioned water pipe system for bathrooms. A little of the old, a little of the new.

Car doors slammed shut and she turned to see her best friend, Raven, and her two dragon mates Frost and Ice—and a woman she recognized but couldn't remember her name—step away from an SUV. Juliet leaned forward and held her stomach to give Raven a hug while the guys headed for the back of the truck.

"You're as big as I was," her friend said, eyeing her belly, "and I had dragons."

Tevrik stepped behind her, twined his fingers under her extended stomach and lifted slightly. Oh god, that helped so much. She didn't have to lean backward to keep from falling forward.

"Yeah, well," Tevrik said, smiling at the arriving group, "wolves are better than dragons any day."

Standing at the back of the truck, Frost hollered,

"I heard that, wolf boy. I dare you to a flying contest any time."

Raven turned to introduce the woman who looked familiar. "Juliet, this is Gerri Wilder, matchmaker extraordinaire."

The memory from a year ago came back to her. "Gerri! I remember you. Good to see you again."

"Wait," Tevrik said, "I've heard that name before."

Gerri shook hands with them and said to Tevrik, "I believe Frost was a middle man between us."

Juliet glanced at the two. "Frost was what?" she asked.

Gerri smiled at her. "I had Frost tell your mate that he should meditate and see what might fall into his lap."

Tevrik leaned back laughing hysterically. Juliet gave him a look that asked *what?* He kissed her hair and said he'd tell her later.

A worker holding a plaque approached. "Excuse me, Alpha. Where do you want this to go for now?" He pulled the paper covering the front. The sign read Brinkley Park.

"Just set it inside the trailer. Thank you, Robert," her mate answered. The jovial air toned down with the solemn memento.

"Ah," Gerri said, "Raven filled me in on the tragic happening as well as how you two met. Simply more proof that things happen for a reason."

Juliet felt Tevrik stiffen behind her. "I have to disagree with you, Ms. Wilder. I see no reason for the death of that innocent child."

Gerri's head tilted and her brow cocked. "No?"

"No, ma'am," he said. Juliet noted the slight anger in his voice only someone who knew him would hear.

"Well, as I understand it," Gerri remarked, "if the Brinkley child hadn't died, then you wouldn't have gone off to learn how to live off the land, and your pack would not have been able to sustain itself as they are now."

Juliet thought that was an amazing insight.

"Plus," Gerri continued, "you wouldn't have been there to save Juliet in the avalanche. You never would have met her. And the gold she found allows your pack to rebuild and have a second chance at sharing the planet with the original inhabitants. So, see? A reason for everything."

Tevrik was speechless. Juliet reached up and closed his hanging jaw. She said, "I believe you are correct, Ms. Wilder. I guess I owe you a fee for finding the perfect man for me."

Gerri laughed. "No worries, dear. I don't charge

for bringing love into this world. But if you're still looking for a name for your child, perhaps I could suggest one that is gender neutral." She winked and headed back to the SUV.

The two guys, Frost and Ice, finally stepped away from the back of the truck. They were dressed in rugged clothing and wore hardhats with a light on the front. They carried pickaxes, and fabric bags were strapped to their belts.

"What are you two doing?" Juliet asked.

Raven rolled her eyes. "When Frost visited your mate last year, he heard some weird story about a kitty leaving a treasure trove of gold in the mountains somewhere. And dragons and treasure are meant to go together. So. . ."

The guys walked up behind Raven and snuggled against her. Frost said, "Yup, we're going to find that hidden loot or die trying."

Juliet glanced up at Tevrik, smiling. At the same time, they said, "Good luck."

THE END

ABOUT THE AUTHOR

New York Times and USA Today Bestselling Author
Hi! I'm Milly Taiden. I love to write sexy stories
featuring fun, sassy heroines with curves and growly
alpha males with fur. My books are a great way to
satisfy your craving for contemporary or paranormal
romance with action, humor, suspense and happily
ever afters.
I live in Florida with my hubby, our boys, and our fur
children Speedy, Stormy and Teddy. I am seriously
addicted to chocolate and cake.

I love to meet new readers, so come sign up for my newsletter and check out my Facebook page. We always have lots of fun stuff going on there.

SIGN UP FOR MILLY'S NEWSLETTER FOR LATEST NEWS!

FIND OUT MORE ABOUT MILLY TAIDEN HERE:

Email: millytaiden@gmail.com
Website: http://www.millytaiden.com
Facebook: http://www.facebook.com/millytaidenpage
Twitter: https://www.twitter.com/millytaiden

If you liked this story, you might also enjoy the following by Milly Taiden:

Sassy Mates / Sassy Ever After Series

Scent of a Mate *Book One*
A Mate's Bite *Book Two*
Unexpectedly Mated *Book Three*
A Sassy Wedding *Short 3.7*
The Mate Challenge *Book Four*
Sassy in Diapers *Short 4.3*
Fighting for Her Mate *Book Five*
A Fang in the Sass *Book 6*

Also, check out the **Sassy Ever After World on Amazon at <u>mtworldspress.com</u>**

A.L.F.A Series
Elemental Mating *Book One*
Mating Needs *Book Two*
Dangerous Mating *Book Three*
Fearless Mating *Book Four*

Savage Shifters

Savage Bite *Book One*
Savage Kiss *Book Two*
Savage Hunger *Book Three*
Savage Wedding *Book Four*

Drachen Mates
Bound in Flames *Book One*
Bound in Darkness *Book Two*
Bound in Eternity *Book Three*
Bound in Ashes *Book Four*

Federal Paranormal Unit
Wolf Protector *Federal Paranormal Unit Book One*
Dangerous Protector *Federal Paranormal Unit Book Two*
Unwanted Protector *Federal Paranormal Unit Book Three*

Paranormal Dating Agency
Twice the Growl *Book One*
Geek Bearing Gifts *Book Two*
The Purrfect Match *Book Three*
Curves 'Em Right *Book Four*
Tall, Dark and Panther *Book Five*
The Alion King *Book Six*
There's Snow Escape *Book Seven*

Scaling Her Dragon *Book Eight*

In the Roar *Book Nine*

Scrooge Me Hard *Short One*

Bearfoot and Pregnant *Book Ten*

All Kitten Aside *Book Eleven*

Oh My Roared *Book Twelve*

Piece of Tail *Book Thirteen*

Kiss My Asteroid *Book Fourteen*

Scrooge Me Again *Short Two*

Born with a Silver Moon *Book Fifteen*

Sun in the Oven *Book Sixteen*

Between Ice and Frost *Book Seventeen*

Scrooge Me Again *Book Eighteen*

Winter Takes All *Book Nineteen*

Also, check out the **Paranormal Dating Agency World on Amazon or at mtworldspress.com**

Raging Falls

Miss Taken *Book One*

Miss Matched *Book Two*

Miss Behaved *Book Three*

Miss Behaved *Book Three*

Miss Mated *Book Four*

Miss Conceived *Book Five (Coming Soon)*

FUR-ocious Lust - Bears

Fur-Bidden *Book One*

Fur-Gotten *Book Two*

Fur-Given Book *Three*

FUR-ocious Lust - Tigers

Stripe-Tease *Book Four*

Stripe-Search *Book Five*

Stripe-Club *Book Six*

Night and Day Ink

Bitten by Night *Book One*

Seduced by Days *Book Two*

Mated by Night *Book Three*

Taken by Night *Book Four*

Dragon Baby *Book Five*

Shifters Undercover

Bearly in Control *Book One*

Fur Fox's Sake *Book Two*

Black Meadow Pack

Sharp Change *Black Meadows Pack Book One*

Caged Heat *Black Meadows Pack Book Two*

Other Works
Wolf Fever

Fate's Wish

Wynter's Captive

Sinfully Naughty Vol. 1

Don't Drink and Hex

Hex Gone Wild

Hex and Kisses

Alpha Owned

Match Made in Hell

Alpha Geek

HOWLS Romances
The Wolf's Royal Baby

The Wolf's Bandit

Goldie and the Bears

Her Fairytale Wolf *Co-Written*

The Wolf's Dream Mate *Co-Written*

Her Winter Wolves *Co-Written*

Contemporary Works
Lucky Chase

Their Second Chance

Club Duo Boxed Set

A Hero's Pride

A Hero Scarred

A Hero for Sale

Wounded Soldiers Set

If you enjoyed the book, please consider leaving a review, even if it's only a line or two; it would make all the difference and would